Contents

10/17/13

To Eerie:
How blessed I
am, to have you
back in my
Life!
Love,
Roberta

My Stories

Roberta Markbreit

PORTLAND • OREGON
INKWATERPRESS.COM

*Scan this QR Code
to learn more about
this title*

Publisher: Inkwater Press

Paperback
ISBN-13 978-1-59299-856-2 | ISBN-10 1-59299-856-9

Kindle
ISBN-13 978-1-59299-857-9 | ISBN-10 1-59299-857-7

Printed in the U.S.A.
All paper is acid free and meets all ANSI standards for archival quality paper.

3 5 7 9 10 8 6 4 2

This is the promise I made to the person I was thirty-nine years ago, when I wrote these stories from a trusting, hopeful heart.

YEARNING

The Errand

I HAD WALKED THIS WAY FOREVER, AND YET IT SEEMED THAT I WAS OUT in the open for the first time.

I inhaled the air: crisp and mellow, tinged with coolness. Little distant wisps, far off clatters, elevated sighs were heard stirring. Stiff leaves shaped like claws whirled at my shoulders, then rushed to settle downward onto the sidewalk. I lowered my eyes. Iridescent stars in the pavement hid as I moved forward and then I turned backward to catch their glints.

Oh, oh, the outdoors! It felt wonderful! I leaned my face into the wind and it thrashed against me, then slid in curves over my nose, my lips, my chin. My hands lifted outward effortlessly, floating. The smooth cadence went on and on. The hum of my walking—one—-two—-one—-two—-surrounded me.

I heard nothing else. A woman with short hair in a red sleeveless dress was bending into the driver's seat through the space of an opened car door, her wide, sagging rump wrinkled from side to side in thick accordion pleats. I imagined the sounds she would be making. The grocery bags she was leaning over would crunch in nervous bursts; soon the car door would slam as though a child had yelled out and had been unexpectedly slapped into silence.

I strained to hear what I thought would be the stiff gray barks of slender trees croaking as they curled upward. Heart-shaped leaves on their outstretched limbs tousled, the greenness of some enduring, and I thought I could hear the blowing of their wind.

Then I heard the inner softness of my body's echoes: vibrations of my ears; the jogging weight of my body in air; the hairs on my head swishing, bobbing; my eyelashes flicking against the brightness of the day.

"Stoooooop!" "Pleeeeeeease!"

I walked on swiftly, refusing to turn around. My large shadow ran ahead of me; the sunshine between the trees made patterns of lace on the narrow throbbing sidewalk. I wanted to keep on going over the hill and on over the next, into the cool, blue horizon.

The boy ran after me. I turned to look. Through the mist, he emerged, his hands fluttering up against the wind, his cheeks flushed, from pursuing me. I saw him in slow motion, graceful, his child's silken knees in flight as pure as his round porcelain face. When he came closer, I felt, as my own, the persistent tickling sensation of the ends of his curly black hair against his delicate ears.

"Come back, come back!" he wailed within the wind. I could not bear his shouting.

All the lightheartedness inside me disappeared. I realized that I could not recapture the day. The air was now cold, unfriendly. The space around me was a shroud of lifeless air. I shuddered, trying to flutter the trembling inside me away. I walked even more hurriedly now, as if I had an unpleasant errand to perform.

All of a sudden, sounds became magnified, jogging me into sensibility. As I passed by, the woman in the red dress scratched her rump and the cotton whispered; the wrinkled nylon slip swished as it hung unevenly underneath the rising hem. She slammed the car door closed. Bam! Then, the motor rumbled. Rh-h-o-o-o-a-a-a-r-r-r!

My sacred silence was no more.

I rushed onward. I began to feel deep pity for the boy that made the bottom of my stomach burn; I knew that no matter how fast he ran and how slow I walked, he would never catch me. I pretended that I could not hear him. My ankles and my calves strained as I hurried to accomplish my errand.

He was crying, crying, why did I have to hear him cry?

I came to the small grocery store, with sheets of glass on either side of its little cavernous entrance, its door lost in shadow. Wooden bins were stacked neatly, with tissue petals blooming between the cubes that overflowed with taffeta-red apples sprouting stiff antennas and glowing suns of grapefruits. In a large corner, cardboard boxes were stacked like cups in a cupboard. Facing me on the other side of the glass, warm neon letters welcomed me.

Inside, the owner ambled aimlessly. He was a tall, thin man, pale and slightly bald, with a thin serrated moustache under a long, slender nose. Over a plaid shirt he wore a white, full-length frock that slid back and forth, scraping his dull brown shoes.

He set a yellow pencil in back of his ear and went to the bananas in the window. With clean, long grocer's fingers he jabbed at the brown dimples curving on the tough mellow skins in a clipped, calculated pace and then stroked them. All the fruits and vegetables were set aright, and they remained implacable after his touch. Satisfied, he began to wander leisurely once again.

He turned, his kind brown eyes looking in pride and honesty at me. Questioning: May I serve you? The neon colors and the translucent glass of the windows warmed us. We confronted each other, friends.

I came out of the grocery store. The boy was waiting for me beyond the threshold. I stood, holding the tall paper bag under my chin and searched his face. Little vague waves, too serious for a boy, undulated on his forehead; his chest rose and fell in short, final gasps.

His eyes looked up, into my soul. The throbbing inside me began again, something melted inside me. I recognized the perfection of youth: innocence, eagerness, trust.

I was crying. I put the bag clumsily down beside me inside the shade of the small cavernous entrance, bending stiffly to do so. The small square tins and tall bottles clattered against the pavement.

'Someday this boy will be a man like you,' I said to myself.

"Now, now," I said aloud, "I was once a child, like you."

Instantly, his fright disappeared. He smiled a little, his black eyes richly alive. He moved to me, his face level with mine as I crouched.

"Don't cry, Pappá, don't cry, I have found you at last!"

His fingers stroked my coarse cheek and dabbed the wetness playfully. I set my head clumsily onto his little shoulder. He touched the top of my head, his hand drowning in the thickness of my hair. We hugged one another, and he stretched his arms 'round to pat my back, he touched my chin, squeezed my neck.

We stayed like that, crouched to the cement, until the grocer opened the door to close shop for the day.

photo credit Guy Nicol

Lily

JUDITH LOOKED UP FROM HER LABORS, STRETCHING UPRIGHT, unwinding the growing strength in her back, her hand wrapped onto the tip of her pole. The succulent ocean-blue sky was limitless, its pure white clouds billowing in rapture. She bent down again. Her rake made short and swift measured movements over the blanket of Winter's dry earth, and gentle red-brown waterfalls of it squirted perfectly through the spaces between the prongs.

In June, she thought, the ground will be leveled and then flooded to welcome the young prickly plants that will grow until they blend into a panorama of vast blue-green that will soar to the edge of the sky beyond where the field seems to end. And then in September, the field will be blazing yellow and there will be richly pink flowers strutting through the fresh green that grows alongside its brazen color.

With the back of her hand, she wiped the wet heat from her forehead. Her arm muscles ached sweetly. Work within the powerful sun was glorious, joyful. She looked forward to the exhausting trudge homeward that would fill her heart with expectancy for the start of the following day.

'Tonight,' she mused, 'Thom's smooth pungent skin will smell beautifully clean, his body against mine. Kissing his arm in the dark, the rain falling thickly outside, I will gently bite a piece of it and his skin will be sweet, firm. My tongue will water as if little gentle knives were running all along the sides of it.'

She looked forward to harvest time, when the water is drained and the field turns pale as ecru and then is transformed into a blanket of lacquered yellow, and the sheaves of harvested rice dry at the edges of all the fields, resembling dancers swirling feverishly in long wide crinoline skirts with their delicate heads aloft, balanced like the true ballet performers that they are.

Each dawn, Judith looked up at the sky instinctively as she and Thom paused in front of the little red door of their peasant home, her eager gray eyes reflecting the faraway mountains drenched in fog, sated with trees that faithfully turn blue when the sun breaks through to start the day. He watched her; then his eyes followed her direction. The thin air emanating from the morning's dew was intoxicating. They smiled trustingly as they waited to enter the familiar body of farmers hurrying to the fields.

It was all unnatural and awkward in the beginning. She was the outcast, the immigrant. Judith's height and light skin blared in a sea of short workers with beige complexions. Her long, neat, dark-blond braid growing all the way down her back from under the peculiar wrinkled hat, her large thin hands and bony wrists floating like butterflies beyond the sleeve ends of her quilted gray jacket, and the sharp ankles poking out of the black pantaloons over the canvas slippers tied with string all made her ripe for ridicule.

In defense against their derisive stares, she felt her arm and leg muscles surging underneath as proof of her worthiness; she wanted to shout out loud the lifelong feeling of joy, the pride, in being born a natural athlete.

She watched carefully. She saw that the women wore oddly shaped straw hats as protection from the relentless, beating rays of the sun as they crouched side-by-side in a singular rhythm as if there were music accompanying their precise movements. With one hand, they each planted the square of rice seeds gingerly and patiently, the other hand filled in readiness to be gently lowered next, over and over and over again.

In kindness, someone had given her a large chimney-shaped straw bonnet with its low wide brim, and it was then that she felt that the floppy wrinkled canvas hat that she had brought in earnest was absurd.

Her sense of certainty blossomed when she was still wanting and hoping for a place to settle into. At the end of a day, the sun closed its eyes after its infinite rays had soaked relentlessly down deep into the moist land and had persistently covered Judith's cheeks, in spite of the wide brim of a borrowed straw hat. On the narrow road that led back to her temporary abode, her eyes lingered on a small-boned woman coming toward her. As they were about to pass one another closely on the narrow path, she was struck by the solemn confidence showing on her face as one hand easily gripped a pole with skirts of raw dried rice plants at either end and balanced gently at the back of her neck, her innate strength defying the size of her. She wore a set of trousers and a long-sleeved turtle necked top of a thin fabric colored in charcoal, an outfit that might be admired by the copies of it back home across the continent, the image amusing her. Here, the pure contentment of her being began to infuse her veins, her bones, her breathing.

It was not always so. Hoping to banish the insistent, lasting feeling of being set apart, she pretended to share with her college friends their passion for material things, which instead only created a more palpable loneliness.

Sheila, the leader of the clique, had planned a bold journey to China, far away over the cusp of the globe, a country that they had studied in their freshman classes in Asian history, drawn to it by bold reds in brightly colored photographs snapped by privileged visiting American exchange students, where very few had traveled. Judith had hoped to gain some joy from it, an exotic place, an alien country.

When they arrived at The Great Wall at sunset, the brick steps going down were soaked in deep-sea blue; beyond, the mountains against the sky carried the blueness aloft. In-between, straight ahead, because the sun had not yet made its final journey into dusk, a solid yellow ribbon sprawled onto a section where the blue ended, parallel to the terraced rice field that began up close and bounced over the hill, never stopping. Up and over and down the large hills the mighty concrete steps soared, halting where the castled forts interrupted, and then moved on.

Looking down and away to her left, Judith saw that there was another set of intimate climbing steps where the milling tourists were reduced to black dots crawling upward, interspersed with red ones that popped like the last gesture of a detailed painting.

The muffled sound of her throbbing heart rose as she began to feel less and less a tourist, even though she stood still alongside her circle of friends. The vast expanse of air began to free her.

To Ling Lee, their personal guide, the group expressed a passionate wish to return to various sections of The Great Wall so that they could watch the nuances of light at various times of the day.

Ling Li's narrow eyes squinted. He wore a casual and neat yellow linen shirt with vague leaves patterned across it and light pockets on the front in which, on their daily routes, he often deposited little maps. He was very comfortable escorting these bright-eyed American women who craved as much history as he could offer in such a short time.

Right away, he saw that Judith stood out from the rest: her body tense and hesitant, the way she stepped outside the circle where her friends stopped and bunched together to look at things, her in-depth questions and keen observations. She approached him surreptitiously, at the ends of lectures and tours, asking him quietly to follow her into the solitary shade under awnings and archways and cliffs, in increments confessing the yearning, the longing, her sense of entrapment. He would advise her, help her, he said.

On the second-to-last day of their trip, at The Great Wall that divided China from the rest of the world, under the warmth of an afternoon sun at the bottom of thin steps that led into the darkness of a fort, the American alums stood stunned by the aloof repose on their friend's face. Sheila, Jean, Shirley, Lila, all were always convinced that their college friend was uncomplicated, friendly, sweet, caring of others. Cautious and frightened, they intuitively backed up against the ancient bricks as if defending themselves against Judith and Ling Li, who were facing them, braced for their reactions.

Ling Li seemed so thin and bony all of a sudden, thought Judith, a severe contrast to the slender, gracefully dressed American women who were ever clad comfortably in soft and sophisticated fabrics that followed the curves of their bodies elegantly. Did any of them feel the fright thundering inside of her from head to toe at her daring? She was convinced that she appeared to them as spare and frail, like a reed struggling to sway in the wind. Did they mistakenly suspect that she had been brainwashed? Even right there, she knew that she would always remember whispering to herself, almost moving her lips: 'If only they'd understand.'

Impulsively, she moved toward them. They embraced stiffly.

She accompanied Ling Li to a cabin made of raw pale logs carefully cut and stacked, with a roof of neat tiers of parched grass going upward, and on either side a little space of a window with two dark twigs crossed inside it that constituted its panes, secured by a frame made of raw clay.

A new kind of relief flowed through her being when she entered to find a large sprawl of floor made of bare wood with no furniture on it, only strange mattresses neatly spaced. Ling Li had told her that she would share the one-floor structure with other women who came from places that Judith could only imagine, who would work alongside one another, preparing to meld into rural life. She was eager and ready for the unknown future, whatever it brought.

Gradually, Judith found it easy in connecting with her bare feelings for the first time in her life. Eventually, within the mass of humanity, and from a distance, she discovered Thom walking to the fields. Soon, he was working alongside her. With clear and unburdened hearts, they fell in love and began to belong to one another.

After a brief ceremony, their lives began in a new house of pale white stucco, with a red door on the front and next to it a window of many small panes. She and Thom cut red and black papers into symmetrical designs to put a circle on the window and a triangle onto the door, and panels with thick Chinese writings in raw black ink on either side of it and above the threshold.

Judith delighted in the simplicity of her new life, in a sparsely decorated house with unadorned furniture handed down to them by family members. Onto the large stark wall in the broad main room they carefully placed a landscape painting with pure brash colors of red flowers on a wide bluish green lawn in front of a blue lake that reflected a simple white building in the distance and a pink tree that blossomed eternally overlapping in the foreground. The colorless white walls were the backgrounds for shiny cylinders of red lanterns and chandeliers dripping with red teardrops that settled at eye level from the ceilings.

Their sole luxury, filling an entire wall, was a console of deep reddish wood inlaid with scenes of gold and spaces sprawled across it for a tiny television set and vases and urns, an extravagant family heritage that spoke of hopes for a long and hearty married life.

After a vigorous day of penetrating the Earth as if for the first time in pointed thrusts and dips and turns, its sweet, moist aroma tapping their daily resurgence of energy, they made the robust tread on the well-worn path toward home.

They halted abruptly in front of their door to find two uniformed men waiting for their return. There was a short, muscular man with a round face and close-cropped hair; the other man was a little taller and thin, with a long, narrow face, his shiny hair swept back neatly behind his ears. Except for the differences in color, one green, one blue, their military dress was identical: a flapped pocket on either side of the chest and a larger set above the hem of the jacket, each on either side of the row of black buttons. In spite of the differences in their physical makeup, their statures were identical: hands efficiently stacked behind their backs at the waist, eyes vacant, their faces parched of emotion.

Judith and Thom went inside, the thin door opening easily. The men followed. They all stood expectant in a casual circle with the front window at their backs. The stocky man's black eyes glittered from the subtle rays of late afternoon coming through the many-paned front window, causing lines of shadow across his face. The taller, thin man nodded imperceptibly, his dark, curious eyes darting occasionally at the gold inlaid console filling the entire wall.

Judith expected this invasion of privacy and almost didn't mind. As a polite bystander she watched their faces. They spoke officially to Thom, only, ignoring her.

Then, automatically, they turned to face her, as if suddenly becoming aware of her presence. She answered yes. Her brief, recent history was given. I'm Lily now, she offered, almost poetically.

Yes, the officials would always come, from time to time, and ask questions, perhaps for the rest of her life.

But this was home. Thom is now everything to me—my world— she offered to herself silently, a gift of repose. She had toiled her whole life to secure the tranquility now felt so completely. Brick by brick, and now: Peace. Yes, this was home. Forever.

I am the Gorilla

I sit. I am lonely. There is the oxygen of silence, everywhere. The floor is flat, hard and cold. Hard light blares, but is warm. The wide glass in front of me has bars outside it. I have learned to look through the spaces. Humans in back of it twist their lips and arms and necks. I cannot communicate my confusion. When I stare at the ceiling or the wall, their smiles heighten and their bodies whimper. When I turn my back to scratch my rump, feeling exposed, or, facing the glass, look down and play with my genitals, one by one, the silent humans bend and gyrate. My furred skin on my buttocks stretches and crackles and is painful.

I sit uncomfortably in water or drying grease left over from feeding time. Then the humans are still, poker-faced, their mouths partly open. Some move from behind the group of them and bump into those in the front rows, or tap the shoulders of others with their fingertips in familial recognition. Then others smile slightly, or laugh. Many have hands in their pants pockets, and stare, hypnotized. Child-humans in the background run ferociously in and out of the lines of the bigger, staring humans.

A blaring, fly-infested ceiling light glows, and shadows of my minutest movements are large and tall along the walls and floor.

I sigh, look up. I am depressed and frustrated. Memory prompts me to reach to a large tree branch, and then, I remember. I feel an incomparable sadness. I place my arm back on my soft belly.

The silence continues.

Finally, after sitting and picking fleas from my chest, my navel, my shoulder, around to my rump, the boredom snowballs to intolerable frustration and I can be inactive no longer. I reach up again and pull on a rubber tire hanging next to me. It sways slightly. The rope attached to it goes through a cage that is along the ceiling. The rope trembles. More humans have gathered in neat, still rows, their faces lining the window. I look into the darkness above them and see less of it as more and more come to watch.

I am cautious, deliberate. I grab the rope mightily, pulling myself up. My other arm sways carefully. Feeling useless, I slide down the rope, its prickly texture making friction all along on my side. Now I stand and stare. My arms and legs bend slightly. My chest rises and my head is high. I hesitate, wait, look.

I become mischievous, rebellious. I reach up with both arms, my eyes directed covertly at the humans. I leap, without momentum, in a perfected stance. My hands spread massively and carefully around an iron log suspended between the walls and riveted through them. In huge scamperings I sway to the right, to the left, all along the log, from one wall to the other, back and forth. I watch the humans carefully, twisting my neck. My legs leap in huge circles as I rock; my hands weave carefully.

Now the crowd is huge and animated. Humans from other windows come over, push and shove, making the rows sway in unison. Now I hear rumbling within the eternal silence. The glass quivers. A large globe of brightness is on the window, and I see rolling heads on either side of it.

I am helpless. I am darkly devastated. I stop swinging and drop onto the flat cement and the bottoms of my feet pound mercilessly onto the hard coldness and then sharp lightning soars up to my knees. I look deeply and childishly into the crowd. My mouth is firm. I am still.

I urinate. I am ashamed. The translucent yellow flow splashes enormously onto the floor. The crowd shivers. Mouths are wide, eyes are glazed, watered, the entire body of humans shakes heavily as one. The glass quivers harder.

Now clumps of feces drop into the urine that is crawling, amoeba-like, in rivulets to spread over the dark cement. One, two, three—four—five. It is done.

The urine splatters and drenches the bottoms of my feet, furthering the humiliation. I wait, again, arms and legs slightly bent, in a vacant stance. I blink. The humans roar in unison and now the glass wavers unceasingly. My humiliation is deep, now. I feel rage. The crowd stops.

I push my mammoth toes against the cold floor. The crowd steps back. I leap; my head tilts to allow my shoulders to hit the glass first. Chest, hips, torso, flying legs, come after, and there is the—SLAP—against the window! The glass is hard against me, my bones rattle. The crowd scatters wildly.

I bounce back from the glass. Erratic noises reach me as I sprawl on my back: twitterings, screeches, roars, howls. I see the expanse of squares that make up the ceiling. My chest heaves; I gasp hugely. My throat is clogged, my ears scream. The floor is cold, hard. I turn my head heavily, and very slowly. The entire darkness beyond the window is now filled with heads of many sizes.

I feel panic, which increases my determination. Now I struggle to rise. I stand to face the glass. My deep brown eyes glitter; my rubber lips part to reveal widely set teeth.

Again, with no momentum, I spring to the window, my entire spread-eagled body hitting the glass all at once. I am, for an instant, pinioned to it. The glass is thick and cold. It undulates heavily.

I drop back to land hard on my feet, and my heels sting, my insides fall. I collapse on my rump. It is hopeless. My hands drop between my knees, near my crotch. My chest still heaves, my mouth hangs open and my tongue protrudes hotly through my chattering teeth.

Suddenly, a piercing cold wetness plunges all over me. My eyes ache to open. The water covers the window, too, and runs massively down the glass. Shapes are blurred, grey. I make out elongated heads, squelched bodies.

I am defeated, infinitely humiliated, massively exposed. I half-rise, and crawl in long strokes on all fours. I lope, right arm, left arm, left leg, right leg. Slowly and deliberately, my knuckles grinding into the cement, I crawl to the far corner, and sit. I am despondent. I maneuver my rump this way and that to get far into the crook of the salmon-painted, splattered walls. I must lower my dignity, far, far.

The water has fallen down the window. Shapes waver. The crowd re-forms in small groups. The humans give me paralyzed looks.

I am apathetic. I sit, I stare. My belly hangs between my knees. I pick up an empty banana peel that is laying nearby and fan it in half circles. A scattering of humans, here and there, attempt to laugh, with restless uncertainty, at my feeble playfulness.

The crowd, larger than before, comes back to border the window. Biting water drips excruciatingly from the roof of my forehead, my fingers, my elbows. The mound on the top of my head is drenched, and aches, too.

The human eyes are hard, and glitter. My despondency grows. The humans move closer to one another, and form rows again. They roar, their arms move, their heads jerk wildly.

I stare for a moment, then a curtain seems to fall thickly over my eyes. There is a glowing devastation inside me. My head lowers; I pick a flea off my knee. My bottom lip curls. Human echoes reach me from a distance.

The glass quivers. I look up to see the human pantomime: the arms flung in air, the twisted mouths, the shiny, even teeth. There is a thickness inside me that drops, my heart falls. My chin flops onto my chest. The banana peel squirms from my fingers and splashes onto my stomach.

There is silence, now. Eternal silence.

In Memory of Bushman,
Lincoln Park Zoo
In Outrage of Zoos Everywhere

Summer Camp

Inside, the heat was still, stifling. The girls gasped softly while lounging on cots or on the wooden floor, cradling their knees or letting their arms drop limply in an unfamiliar exhaustion. The tufts of hot blankets on the cots scratched the backs of their bare legs when they straightened them out to find comfort and relief. The dark green floor shimmered dully and was sticky all along their legs and hard against their bones as they stretched as far as they could to calm their sweltering nerves. Everyone else was gone.

Through the screen all along the cabin wall, the sun was magnetically hot and bright. The hill was a sweeping fan of green across the sky.

Through a dark corner, a girl rose. Her arms flowed as she crossed to the far side of the room where a young girl stood leaning against the shiny frame of the opening to the wide, empty center room lined with open cubbyhole spaces. She turned slowly as the only motion in the room approached her as her own pale eyes became mesmerized by the long thin neck and the beautiful blue vein throbbing through the clear skin. The girl came to her and dipped her chin to rest her head against the young girl's shoulder.

She said then, "I love you." She raised her head and kissed the silken neck. Silence was so still that it whistled in the heat.

"I've wanted to tell you this for some time," she whispered. Her gray eyes roved slowly over the pale face.

The girl stayed still against the frame of the doorway, her eyelids closing deeply.

The one who had ventured across the room buried the fullness of her lips into the curved edge along the thin neck, above the shoulder, settling them there, for always.

Cattle

THE NIGHT WAS COOL, WITH THE DISTANT, HIDDEN HEAT MAKING promises. Apartment buildings jutted out of the depth of early evening because of their darkness being only a pale hue away. Window screens, like sieves, spanned bay windows of warmly lit living rooms, creating modern impressionist paintings to look up to; even the subdued lilting chatter of families beyond them flowed through to hang in the air high over pale streets not yet settled into the curtain of evening darkness. Trees swayed listlessly, expectant.

With no one else on the street, a tight clique of girls owned the evening. Familiarly patterned, the marching group consisted of three rows, each row set with best friend matched to best friend, two-by-two, with the leader and her sidekick solid at the front.

Their arrangement was meant to seem spontaneous, but it was tacitly plotted. There was a studied laziness in the way they stayed together. The leader set the stage, turning backward; walking, walking, her knees dipping languorously, expertly; then, turning to face forward, keeping to the beat. Shoulders bumping. Thighs bumping. One in the second row jerked to a stop to pull up a twisted bobby sock while her best friend stopped to wait; the rest tripped all over one another.

The leader's looks were common: round brown eyes, a round face, dark curly hair cropped to just under her ears. The members worshipped her. Although not brilliant, she took charge from the beginning, since fourth grade, and that gave the rest comfort in her directing them.

There was a lump of tenderness that kept growing in the girl in the last row. Tonight, she could feel it in the strange promise in the prickly air. The street lamps made glittering dots in the eyes of her friends, eyes that had become slowly and surely alien to her after all these years. Now, especially in the early evening's darkness, she recognized the hard truth in their smiles as their teeth gleamed with their small-mindedness, their instinctive meanness.

Suddenly, there was the muffled clatter of heavy, fleeing feet stumbling frantically. The air lifted and then, emptiness. Now, they were all gone, swept away. They were retreating clumsily ahead of her; there were thick, muffled giggles, a consent, a plan unknown to her, a plot that frightened her. She would run, too, not understanding why; perhaps because someone was chasing her. The impenetrable darkness that had surrounded her closed in.

"Hello, Serena."

An innocent greeting made her swiftly turn her head as the girl came up silently from behind to reach her. Under the streetlights, her round face and piercing brown eyes beamed for a moment.

"Hell—o, Dorothy."

Serena's eyes shot into the distance, and she saw the blot of bobbing heads, the bumping of legs creating flashes of light between them. The cloud of hilarity was softened by the distance, and the herd of cattle evaporated into the night.

'So, they ran from Dorothy.'

The sharpness of this reality popped up and heaviness spread across her heart.

'How could they be so mean?'

Their running was an image that confirmed her separateness; she would never be one of them—ever.

Dorothy's gaze was plain and unblinking as they began to walk side-by-side. Dorothy's trust in her made Serena uncomfortable for its honesty. She stared ahead as they turned to go back, listening to her smooth and guileless chatter, her voice raspy at the edge because of the rising heat. For the first time of knowing her from afar, Serena felt the palpitation of Dorothy as a human being, an individual with deep tenderness, with feelings so similar to her own.

"—How is your mother?" her voice whispered.

Oh, yes. Serena remembered. Dorothy had always had respect and admiration for her family, whom she had met when they had gone to a small private school when they were little. They had even been friends. They were in classes together, had sat bunched in groups, had sat in a row along a bench while they had cut and pasted paper necklaces and drawn with crayons. They had eaten lunches in the dining room on another bench with other classmates between them. They had stood on the large gravel yard in a line, looking up and listening to the teacher at the front, who had placed a firm index finger upright against her tight lips.

She whispered, "Let's pretend we have locked our lips and thrown away the key."

Then she turned her wrist, pinched her lips, and locked them.

"She's fine, thank you—my mother's—fine."

They kept on walking. Serena's mind roved wildly.

"Are you going this way—? I'm going all the way to the corner—."

'It was stupid, what came out.'

"I'll walk with you," Dorothy answered quickly.

They whispered as they walked. School, the assignments, the upcoming trip to the Museum of Science and Industry.

"Who are you going to sit with on the bus?"

Serena halted, her feet gasping against the pavement. Her eyes lingered in the distance and stopped at the point where Dorothy's gaze was set. Dorothy stopped walking, too. Serena turned to face her: the clear brown eyes, the unchanging seriousness. She was confused; she felt slender lines blossoming across her own forehead.

" I don't know."

'Probably my best friend, Judy,' she thought to herself.

She turned back and began walking again, with effort, slowly. She could not stop herself from staring into the blackness. Dorothy turned obediently and walked beside her.

They talked of school, classmates, and their teachers, especially Mrs. Sangerman, the science teacher who was taking them on the trip. Serena took deep breaths and remembered that the high heat had been promising to come into this night, had meant to be special. They came to the corner, then stopped and turned to one another at the same time.

"Well, I have to go now."

Serena lifted her head shortly to indicate the other side of the wide street.

Dorothy stared at her in anticipation with the same steady eyes and full, firm lips. Serena said nothing. She did not want Dorothy to accompany her across the street, or home. She wanted to be alone in the dark, all the way down the long street with the tiny lights glittering overhead. She wanted to walk fast, searching the deeply shadowed cubes of grass next to the curb. The street with the occasional cars coming down it would protect her. Maybe she would walk into the street itself part way like she did sometimes at night, away from the deep caverns of building entrances. The lights from the posts would expose her, keeping her from harm as people watched from the windows. She wanted to be alone, now. She was impatient, and she wanted this walk to stop.

She glanced purposely for the last time at the thick brown eyes, saying, "—Bye," and Dorothy, looking deeply into her shadowy, lamp-lit face and saying, "Bye, Serena," even in goodbye, waiting, watched her run across the wide street, over the sleek, gleaming streetcar tracks.

Serena did not look back when she got across. Dorothy watched as she evaporated into the blackness. Then she turned around and began gingerly retracing their steps. After a short distance, she stopped absently, and went back to the corner. She craned her neck and lifted her head, throwing her voice across the street.

"I'll see you in school," she hollered and the air clung to her words.

The words rose, flinging sharply down the tunneled street. Serena winced at their sounds, forcing a soft thunder to cloud her ears, and her shoulders rose against them as if she were cold. She gathered momentum in her stride, and went on home.

I Love You, Frank Sinatra

I AM EIGHT YEARS OLD. I AM SITTING ON THE FLOOR, FACING THE RADIO, which is set on a very low shelf. Anne, my sixteen-year-old sitter, is with me. We are scrunched up, our knees tight against our chests. She is talking in a low, flowing tone.

It is summer. The air comes through the wide, black-encrusted screen, which spreads across the dining room wall of our second-floor apartment. Particles of soot swirl through it onto the large dining room table, mildly covering the shiny, beautiful wood, making the summer warm and intoxicating. The screen faces the side of the apartment building next to ours; there is the shadowed back porch of the people across the way.

The gangway below and between us creates echoes of vague, light-moving sounds and heavier sounds of feet pounding up and down it every so often, back and forth. The light air lifts me. There is a delightful feeling of not being able to breathe, of light-headiness.

Things around me seem to sparkle: the chandelier light above me, fanning out; the kitchen ceiling, bright from the white porcelain light just beneath it; the wet, sleek cleanliness of the dulled-white kitchen sink. The dishes have just been washed and set carefully in the drainer and the smooth grooves of the porcelain beneath it form channels of clear water that rush silently and drop lightly into the well of the sink. We have just finished dinner and there is the heaviness of recent activity.

Anne is watching the radio and listening intently. I imitate her. The radio is blond wood, tall, bulbous. The dials are at the bottom, dark liquid brown. The screen above them encloses and holds back what is inside, and gives off a soothing warmth of sound in the living room, beyond, on the other side of me.

We are listening to Frank Sinatra, who is singing in a theater. There is an audience of girls—bobby soxers, Anne calls them—who stand and applaud, their eyes hypnotized by the brightness from the stage (my image of them), and then they swoon, which means falling and swaying in ecstasy—fainting—into their seats.

Now, I am there, higher than the balcony, watching. The seats are like those in the movie theaters I've been in: maroon, plush, prickly.

You, Frank Sinatra—.

Now that I am aware, I see you in photos in movie magazines and newspapers. You wear a bow tie under a skinny neck and an Adam's apple in it. Anne explains that this is your trademark. Your hair bubbles against your effervescent face. There are lines like lemon slices around your smile. Those are dimples, Anne says.

A yellow spotlight is all over you as you play with the microphone as though it is a part of you: a caress, a touch. You are holding a woman in your arms.

I am ten years old. I linger at my round dresser mirror, catching patches of my face in glimpses. I watch myself in the long mirror on the closet door of my bedroom. I see myself, but I am always wondering what I am.

I come home right from school, whisking by my mother and her friends as they play Mah Jongg at the card table in the living room. I wander down the hall and into my bedroom; then I rush eagerly into my mother's bedroom.

I take off my school clothes, put on my mother's warm, long green robe and lift my hair up with my arm across the back of my head so that the curls and strands flow over my elbow, down my neck, cascading softly, like silk. I stand in front of the dresser mirror. There is lipstick and rouge on my face. It feels thick, tight. I have put that on, too, somewhere between the robe and the mirror.

I smile at myself in the mirror, I smile at the older me. I seem taller. I feel somewhat hard, different. The deep red fills my full lips so I can see them well. My hair is pinned up, now. Yes, I look like, and therefore am, older. Pretty. I want to look like this in a hurry; I don't want to wait.

I do this every day for a long time. I come home, whisk by whatever is happening in the living room, into my brightened bedroom with the dark heavy furniture and then go into my mother's closet and put on the green robe. There is the yellowish light from outside, through the Venetian blinds; the dark wood; the soft green thick material of the robe against me; my piled-on, fluffy hair. Red lips. Even, pretty teeth. A childishly, seductive smile.

I am twelve years old, now. Boys chase me and my friends down the street, and whisk our patterned silk babushkas off our heads. We careen and turn and chase *them* now and they run heavily and swiftly, 'way ahead of us. It is impossible to catch them; they are expert runners. I am lightly wet and flushed with exhaustion, excitement. I am enormously and childishly frustrated, too, by the longing to have back what is rightly mine. It is all new and deep, what I feel. The sudden, enormous knowledge of their strength—of their bodies running, bodies that are strange in their swift heaviness and depth—confuses me.

Television has been invented. Donny, my twelve-year-old neighbor whom I grow up with, says that we will actually **see** Frank Sinatra singing on the stage. He is sitting at his desk in his bedroom looking up at me and I am in the opposite corner on the top bunk of his beds.

I am walking home from the beauty shop with an older boy under a light Spring rain. Walking with him is strange. I am not accustomed to older boys; he is different, new.

It is grey-dark from the dampness. My hair has just been washed, set in bobby pins and dried, and, therefore, it feels mature; but the rest of me still feels young. My hair doesn't fit, exactly. My legs feel soft because of the rain against them. My skin is cold from the air and the newness of the tall, rough-skinned, older-looking boy. I flow naturally, irresistibly, to the puddles all along the sidewalk and kick aimlessly and gently through them as I walk. It feels right to have the water spread over my galoshes. I fall deep into the rightness of it.

It doesn't feel right to let the rain misshape my carefully done hairdo, but there seems to be no other way. I am not in control. The rain falling light, light, slowly and certainly crumbles the rigid outline and makes the stiffness sag all around my head. My mother has given me an umbrella to use, but the boy so close by my side makes all the difference. It is a wide, huge black umbrella, my father's. It is not right to put it over my head: It would be embarrassing to use what is practical. Practical is absurd. Nervously I swing it, closed, over the puddles, then clutch it to me, feeling helpless. I feel the rain tap, tap, tapping onto my head, pounding lightly, making dents on the rigid, beautiful shape all around the crown of my head. The beauty operator has made the style firm, and beautiful. The silken strands and the shape go limp, heavy, frizzed, falling into a mass, losing the perfect beauty of the shape. I feel the heavy wetness changing the shape.

I feel frantic that everything on my head is going wrong, but I say nothing, having to talk to him and put up a front and pretend not to worry, pretend that nothing wrong is happening, pretend that nothing is being ruined, the time spent to make the perfect hairdo, the money, the achievement of the beautiful appealing ideal shape. All changed in the rain, all ruined, all useless. My head feels limp with the struggle of the hair to maintain its shape. Part of my head still clings to the shape; other patches are limp, fallen. It is all uneven, uncomfortable.

I am trying to maintain my smile, my confidence, my control. I smile for him, do not let him see the darkness inside me like the dampness in the air. Above all, it is necessary to show determination in the face of what is happening, not let him see the ugly struggle of trying to keep the perfect shape intact and it not staying right, he must not see the efforts gone awry. I smile, joke, agree, laugh, flirt. That is what is important.

I go up the stairs through the dark hallway, then into our apartment. It is dark inside. My mother exclaims breathlessly that my hair is ruined and what happened? She flaps the palm of her hand against her cheek and chin. Her mouth is agape, her eyes glazed in mild horror.

I feel wrong, I did it wrong, everything in the world I have done is wrong, it is all wrong. The way I felt walking home is made certain, made real. It is all true, now. There is no question; it was wrong to get so wet. It is irretrievable. I am now convinced that walking home in the rain without the umbrella covering me was terrible to do, messy. I am deep in the tangled mess of the wrongness. There is nothing to do but give up, retreat into the wrong way I did things.

I am a teenager now. I spend summers at a girls' overnight camp. Boys and a completeness of other friends are left behind in the hot bright city. It is all changed in the Summer. Hot, sticky nights and I am restless. I writhe on my neat bed—which I have made for the counselors' inspection—against the hot blanket.

I think of boys so much, and the counselors are strangers, but here they are in front of me, inches away from me, their faces close, close. I am voluptuous inside myself, I tingle. I moon, slump inside myself at I don't know what. I am play-acting but it is real. I am sad. I don't ask myself why, I am just mooning, moaning inside. I am spreading with my deep sadness over everything around me, although no one seems to notice anything different about me.

The lake surrounding our peninsula makes its waves in pointed, silent kisses and it murmurs. It moves my feelings: loves long ago, loves in the future, heartbreak to be done. I grope. I am sentimental, lovesick. I am sensuous. My feelings fly out into the air.

Hot sticky nights. I groan silently, inside myself. I miss the boys. There are smells and textures. I have breathless vitality; I don't know what to do with it. I am lonesome.

I am isolated.

We sprawl on the hard wood floor of the Rec Hall. There is a sheet hanging from across a wire. It is our movie screen. It is hot, sticky. I writhe within the damp legs of my friends, pretending comfort from their love, which I accept but which I do not understand. My curved back is too high along the hard floor. It makes me even more restless.

We look 'way above into the high thick beams, thinking, far away. The legend is that there are bats up in there. Yes, they are there: I saw one swoop in front of the folds of the sheet/screen, in front of the inflated, black and white darting images that seem to fly into the air from the breezes that enter through the large opened doorways. Figures act, react, slide over the folds; the sound booms thickly; often, it is indistinguishable. We intertwine within each other's bodies, gazing, sleepy.

One night, you, Frank—you—appear. The sheet sways. You are singing—"What is America to Me?" Your hands are in your pockets. Your effervescence. Your cascading hair, bright eyes. You— skinny—. Your Adam's apple—. Oh—. Yes—. I remember—.

I am going to college now. I am actually a college coed. I am seventeen.

I lug all kinds of things up the steps of the small hill, into the modern sorority house building. My parents are following behind me, smiling at all the newness. I am smiling, too; I am uncertain inside, but smiling. There are many new friends smiling and the older girl is waiting for me. I am her roommate; she is to be my "big sister." She is eager for me, and her pride in me gives me relief from uncertainty. I am suddenly confident. She makes me feel so special.

I crowd my things into a tiny room of bare, stuccoed walls. My "big sister" has a phonograph—a luxury. It is new, sleek. She flips a switch. No cranking up, no changing sides. There are new, different kinds of records; they revolve slowly, are unbreakable. No more fast 78's that now have vague, tinny sounds and crack if we're not careful. The new sounds are sweet, clear, liquid—alive inside our very room, here, with us.

My roommate stacks the new thin album covers neatly upright. The cover of the record she is playing is on her studio bed. You— Frank Sinatra—lean on a lamppost under a glowing light. Your hat over your eye—your smile—a coat over your shoulder—a cigarette's smoke rising from between your lips.

Down the hall, and around the corner, someone leaves the door to a room open, on purpose, and the halls fill with your new voice. Your voice—you—a mature voice that teases, dips, whirls, twists where the tenderness is raw. There is sweet arrogance, now—. All the old pain and bittersweetness is alive, again; I am *inside* the music. You—. Frank—Sinatra.

I am older, now. Events flow back and forth, and interweave. You—coming back. You, acting in a movie, in a heart-wrenching role that stuns the public. Everyone is suddenly aware and awed by the brilliant, newest You—.

I am getting married.

You, on television, now, a part of all our lives.

I am having children.

You are married again, divorced. Your children are growing up. You have become the entertainer.

Oh, I am turning away—but I do remember—sometimes—I do—.

You have mellowed—.

So have I—.

I loved you, Frank Sinatra.

SUNSHINE

The Wheelbarrow

THE BOY WATCHED HER ALL MORNING. HE WATCHED HER SILHOUETTE as it bent down heavily while she quietly opened the oven door. Only her thick hands were clearly seen in the open window within a panel of brightness as she worked. A large towel sagged between her fists as she groped with experience for the handle, and the foam of sweetness roared softly throughout the kitchen, then wiggled outdoors, to him.

He had followed an aroma that careened over the countryside. Bubbling cherries wafted over him at dawn, as, carpetbag in hand, he tiptoed over the threshold of the orphanage, the place he had called home all his life. Thick, quiet darkness gave way to the struggle of a bright sheet of light, and sparrows twittered incessantly, hungrily. As the crystal dew melted and the tawny, listless leaves dropped new dust, he followed the scent lightly, over the slender path that dipped into moist earth that surrounded houses hugged by thick trees. Leaves had fallen everywhere, making brittle stars over the hills and valley and his light steps made bunches of them scatter noisily.

He wore a pair of blue velvet shorts and a white, ruffled shirt. His shoes were faded brown, but clean. He was not worried about the possibility of cold weather, for by winter, he knew, he would be safe.

All the way through the forest, he thought of the home he had left. He did not want to forget it, ever. He thought of the bleached-brown wooden building, small and square. Wild flowers stuck out from underneath it, blue, yellow ones. It was on the top of a small hill and from its windows he could see over the countryside, all around. He thought of the huge room where he had so recently slept, spare and clean it was, the light coming in through the floor-to-ceiling windows, reflecting onto its wood floor and the tiny dressers. It was carefully filled with many other cots neatly made like his were, and the children who slept in them were all he knew of friends. And the ladies in fresh gingham dresses, bending over him, especially in the morning, to kiss and hug him. He liked to bury his nose inside the crooks of their arms to make their silky skin stay with him all day. Often, all the children would crowd to them at once, pushing them gently for particles of warmth.

Light came through spaces between the leaves overhead to warm his face and make patterns that slid over him like fine lace as he walked and thought. It was cool, otherwise, and the thick dampness was a comfort. He gasped as his way became more narrow and the slender foliage closed in. Every now and then a brittle log crossed his path. He sat down, once, to rest, pulling the bag close to his feet. Birds were settled inside the dark all around him, watching. He looked up to see the sun blaring between the shadowed leaves and branches, so he rose to pick up the bag, then stepped over the log and went on.

There were whispers, and a caw-caw-cawing flung overhead. A branch rustled very close, and his head turned swiftly, but he kept on. He saw the light of day ahead, and soon the heaviness of the forest lifted. The rustling slowly thinned, and in one step he came out.

Immediately the scent of baking apples and peaches rose up, thicker and closer. There were small hills all around, as far as he could see. Purple wildflowers were strewn from the edge of the woods.

A small cottage appeared. It had an enormous dark roof that spread like yeast to hang over and shade the pale stone walls. Windows were carved in it and tiny dark shutters spread outward from them. The front door was partly open to reveal a tall, thick woman in a full white apron using a broom in soft strokes. Stone squares made a path to the door between a garden on either side of it. A large black dog slept on the stone steps in the remaining shade, his paws on either side of his face.

He passed more and more houses with the increasing warmth of the day. Some were like gingerbread with white picket fences around them. Children who played inside the tiny yards waved, and the older ones stared. Other houses had goats on the roofs, eating grass. The restlessness of early morning grew, and he could hear the voices of the children behind him.

He came to a large white house with high windows. The brightest grass he had seen all morning grew right up to it; cobblestones made a path through it from the road. The same purple flowers from the forest found their way here and were splattered all around it. There was a window as tall as the house itself on either side of the front door, like the windows in the orphanage. The door was painted white like the rest of the house, a clean, pure white, and it had black hinges and a partition that cut it in half crosswise.

Beyond the farthest side of the house, a man in a dark shirt and loose trousers sat on an upturned pail and milked a cow. Beyond him, a log fence surrounded a pasture where cows and horses mixed. There were larger hills in the distance, and the boy could see no more beyond them. The sky became its fullest pale blue.

Beyond the side nearest to where he stood, the boy could see a stilled wooden bucket suspended inside a well. Chickens roamed near it and popped out from behind the corner of the house and strutted lazily, and balked.

Old trees all around fanned and shaded like giant umbrellas. There were apple trees, and the oldest stood between the house and the road, in a tiny dale. A bench circled it and apples had begun to fall between the soft blades of grass, apples part green, part deep crimson. Its shade spread to the edge of the cobblestone path.

He longed to fall in a heap under it and reach over to hold a cool, moist apple in the cup of his hot hand. Instead, he ran under the high window at the side of the house and looked up. He could see the undersides of several pie tins that leaned heavily over the edge of the long sill and steam pouring way over the pie mounds, stirring the drowsy air above them. He could tell what kinds of pies they were, one by one, by the smells, as they were lined up to cool: cherry, berry, apple, ginger-peach. The thick delicacy of each went through his nostrils and watered his eyes sweetly.

He could hear the swishings of hands against an apron and soft heel scrapings against a floor. The clink of a spoon settling onto a wooden table to rest, the soft clatter of a pot set on the stove burner. And the now near, now distant heavy, satisfied breathing of someone who had been doing early morning work for a lifetime.

He moved away quietly, and sat down on the pile of carpetbag, opposite the window, his legs crisscrossed in front of him. He chose a spot where the sun made a blaring circle, but the shade from the trees all around bordered it, and he was cool enough. Now, with heavy eyes, he could see the soft shadow in the window, moving about. He could see a full, flushed cheek when the figure sprung and darted smoothly into the panel of sun that came into the open window. Then, the long nose as the silhouette faced the window for an instant, hesitated, and turned back to its work, its back to the outdoors. Sometimes the shadow of the figure was lost in the larger shadow of the kitchen's background, and it became indistinguishable.

Slowly, he made more and more of it out: a white half-apron, thick pastry-encrusted hands, dark uplifted hair. The oven door fell softly, rose and closed thickly—open, shut, all morning.

And just before his head drooped a little, the figure came closest to the window. A full square of brightness made the dark green dress bloom fully in sunshine. It had tiny yellow tulips all over it in neat rows. Buttons down the front, too—. His head fell at last. He dozed.

The lady was pleased and heavy with her work. She moved to the window, then slid her large-boned wrist along her square forehead. She sighed, and surveyed the five pies lined up before her in the sun, steaming heartily. The vapors caressed her large face, blocking, temporarily, the sunny brightness from outside. She sighed, again, in final satisfaction, wrung her hands within her apron skirt, and turned away. In a moment she came back, this time fully visible within the now blazing, late morning sun. Gingerly, a towel between her hands, she placed the final pie at the end of the line, a pungent pumpkin.

She looked up and out, beyond the sill, to rest her eyes.

The boy woke. He heard birds chattering busily. He was startled to see clearly a large woman standing fully in the sunlight from the open window, facing him. Her face was expressionless; then, her eyes widened, slightly startled, and her mouth dropped open. She continued to face him and the longer she stood, the softer and more settled on him her brown eyes became.

The woman first saw the boy flopped on a carpetbag in the very middle of a wide circle of sunlight. She watched him look up, as he was startled out of a dozing sleep. His hair was thick and dark blond as the sun's warmth and brightness reflected onto the top of his head; the ends were slightly moist, and darkest. She saw, even from the distance, the round blueness of his eyes and that they were deep, reflecting the dark blue of his trousers. His face was soft and pure, she could see that, pure because it was such a clear, lovely face, and round cheeks that flushed, almost blazed, with pink. He lay in a kind of heap, legs entwined in outstretched arms that hung over a raised knee.

She forgot her pies, now. The steam had seemed to vanish into the light morning wind. She could not speak.

The boy stumbled as he rose, and wavered on his feet. He came closer to the window, the carpetbag bumping along his heels, as the warm sun woke him fully. He saw the wavy lines melt above the lady's heavy eyebrows. There were crescents around her rich, pale mouth, and tiny indistinct rays circling the dark brown eyes.

Otherwise her skin was smooth; her hair dense and shiny, raised stiffly into a perfect doughnut.

He stopped a short way from the window sill.

"Hello," he said.

His voice was soft but firm.

"Who are you?" the woman asked, in a tone thick and strong, like the rest of her, and a little deep.

"My name is Jamie," he answered, louder, his chin risen to allow his voice to reach her.

"Oh—Jamie—." she imitated weakly, oddly relieved at the boy's identity and the words trailed off as she continued to look at him.

"Yes, Jamie," he repeated, "That is who I am."

"But - -." she resumed, "where—where are you from?"

"I have walked from the orphanage at dawn, through the forest, and through the village, and now I am here!"

He said this as though he had finally arrived at a prearranged, expected destination.

"Oh—." Now her face was softer.

Composing herself by adjusting her shoulders, her thick brows diving inward toward the bridge of her nose, she asked what she assumed would be an unnecessary, and therefore, reassuring question.

"Then—you—know where you are?"

"Not exactly—but—I know this to be the right place."

Her dark, quizzical eyes became distracted. The woman raised her wide chest, and let it fall into the largest sigh she had made all morning. She saw the boy's scuffed shoes, the blinding white shirt, with patches of gray dirt on it.

"Why are you here?" the lady asked, finally.

Jamie answered without hesitation, having waited for that precise question.

"I am here to ask for work."

"Work? What kind of work can you do"?

The boy seemed too young and unscarred to have done much work.

"There is much to do around here—," she quickly added, then regretted it but went on, "—and you are only a small boy."

Jamie's blue eyes roved for the first time to a bright shiny red wheelbarrow he had not seen before that leaned against the back corner of the house.

"Oh—I can bring you—." he said, tentatively at first. "I can bring you —." And he went quickly on, "the SUN, the SUN and its shadows. I can bring the sun and its shadows inside your house for you, so that you shall be comfortable and warm, always."

The lady's shoulders dropped easily, and she threw her head back, in relief, and laughed gustily, deeply. Her eyes squinted beautifully, as though a careful painter's brush stroked them, and small teardrops murmured on the edges of her bottom lids. The boy saw her wide, even teeth.

She straightened up, and now her face was even softer, her eyes twinkling and wet.

"How—how will you bring me the sun?"

"I will bring you pieces of it, in your wheelbarrow." He pointed.

"When the sun is at its fullest, as it is now, I will put the wheelbarrow under the trees, and let the sun that is between the leaves, fall into it."

"Ah-h—." the lady exclaimed, and clapped her hands, "pieces of sun! I always wanted to hold the sun in my hands."

She raised her hand and cupped it, as though waiting for the sun to fall into it.

"Yes," Jamie, reflected, encouraged by her delight.

"And," the lady went on, curious to know more, "what about the shadows? How will you bring me shadows? How will you do THAT?"

Jamie had no immediate answer.

"Well," the lady said, encouragingly, now leaning forward, her palms on the sill, "every time I try to scoop up a shadow in time for dinner, it disappears. Either it rains and the water makes it gray and gone, or the sun moves on and the shadow lengthens and is big, and no matter how far I stretch out my arms, I cannot catch it."

"Well," the boy said, his forefinger now resting on his chin in serious contemplation, and his eyes askance, "I will not only let the <u>sun</u> fall into my wheelbarrow, I will let the shadows do the same."

The answer pleased him.

His answer pleased the lady, too, for she rejoined, her eyes now gleaming softly.

"Oh, that is wonderful! I will be able to make my Puzzle Cake better than ever, now."

And she enraptured about her famous, special cake.

"My Puzzle Cake, made up of several different small cakes baked into one, and eaten by simply tearing off the pieces after it has baked for half a day. Instead of butter and flour and raisins, I will sift and mold and knead the sun and its shadows into a batter of capricious shapes and the most delicious, magical flavors. M-m-m, how good these pieces will be."

As she spoke, she gesticulated with her hands, putting together an invisible Puzzle Cake.

"You said rain."

"What?"

"You said when it rains, the shadow disappears, and you cannot catch it."

"Yes, yes," she said eagerly.

"Well, I can do that, too; I can catch the rain. All I have to do is stand outside with a cup in my hand, and let the rain fall into it."

"Yes, that is nice, that will be easier," she said, gazing abstractedly.

"With as much rain as there is to spare, I can make volumes of my Raindrop Soup. I never make less than volumes of it, anyway, for there is always so much rain to go around. Volumes," she reflected.

Jamie looked now at the volumes of yellow tulips on her dress.

"I will bring you buttercups—," he murmured, almost to himself.

"Ah-h—." She searched his half-closing eyes. "I can make buttercup sauce, then sprinkle it over my bread before I put it into the oven to bake."

She raised her pie-encrusted forefinger for effect and saw that the sun had melted a speck of cold butter that had set onto her fingertip. She licked it off.

The boy noticed that there were white ruffles around the window frame, and his eyes lingered.

She saw that.

He looked away, immediately, and saw sunflowers straight and stiff behind the wheelbarrow, near the edge of the house. He looked farther, and beyond the wheelbarrow and the well and the chickens and the pasture with the log fence that swung around on this near side of the house, he saw the field of cornstalks blowing easily, and high as the sunflowers.

He rambled wearily:

"I will bring you a bushel of ripe, full tomatoes."

"—for my tomato pie—."

"—and peaches from the orchards—."

"—peaches with velvet skins—."

"I will bring you—."

"We shall see—but for now—you must be hungry and tired—."

And the woman, who Jamie was to find out later was named Johanna Beazley, disappeared momentarily from the window. She reappeared by his side, her hands brushing along her apron in front. Her dress came to the toes of her black pointed shoes, and she was tall.

"We shall see," she continued, in a rising, firm voice, "but for now, you must eat, then rest—and—we shall see—we shall see."

With the back of her hand she wiped the remaining wetness from her dark eyes, and she smiled peacefully.

She bent down to clasp his hand and pull him gently to the house, through the front door. She lifted the carpetbag with her other hand, bending, and as she did so she looked into his marble-blue eyes. The transparent lids slowly closed almost all the way over them as he let himself be led.

"Hans! Hans!" she called to the man still milking the cow on the other side of the house.

"Hans! Come quick!"

That night Jamie slept in a room by himself for the first time in his life. The dark wood floor shone from the moon. The pillow was high and soft under his heavy head. The tall window across from his bed was dark blue and speckled with stars. He was full and warm.

As he fell asleep he knew that the winter would come soon and under the trees all would be white and soft.

That night he dreamed of apples in the snow.

Away, Away

THE THREE CHILDREN WERE THERE FROM THE COUNTRY. THEIR SKIN was peach as tea roses, their eyes golden. They were clustered onto the little square of cement, looking up, up, to where their grandmother was. Their bobbing heads rocked back on their necks to follow the gray wooden steps that narrowed, one by one, to the top to see her. They could not see the roof; their eyes screeched to a halt at the ceiling edge under it, smooth and flat, like the top of their mother's chocolate layer cake, and high near the traveling clouds that passed swiftly by and never stopped.

Their grandmother was distant in a thick gray dress that billowed in two parts, from her shoulders to her waist, then, from her waist in a larger amount to the tips of her small black shoes. A rivulet of flat black buttons went down the center of it, from the scoop of the neckline to the wavering hem.

The children danced up the steps in a million ways. Up, up, they jigged, to the landing of the porch at the top. In final, desperate summer gasps they surmounted the wooden floor. Their feet bumped to a stop close to their grandmother. Their faces blanched in greeting her. Their smooth pink mouths formed little circles; then, like ladies' purses clamping prissily shut, their lips tightened in wrinkles, and closed. O, o, their lips seemed to say, and were silent.

Their grandmother rocked in a chair. Her thick face was pale and unyielding. Her hair was brown in a bun at the back of her head. All she said was, over and over,

"Up and down, up and down," meaning them, but, as though they were not there, she gazed through the strata of colorless sky while she said it.

They were careful not to brush against the sacred space around her. They slithered by her, to grab at the screen door; it fell back and clattered behind them as they rushed inside. Through the mesh could be seen tall pure glasses of pale lemonade against their lips. Their eyes bulged through the liquid and searched the distorted bottoms.

"Up and down, up and down," all summer, all day, away, away, from the country, to the city, all day, away.

Dedicated to Rena Beverly Markbreit

Fish Who Fly

LITTLE SAMMY BITTERMAN, FOUR YEARS OLD, SQUIRMED AND WAS being obnoxious, his Mama thought. His dark blond, tightly curled head swayed this way and that in eighty-degree arcs; his arms were rolling all over his chest and he twisted them so that they were all mixed up and inside out. He stomped his feet emphatically, his sneakers making no sound at all. Sammy's efforts went unnoticed over the jabbering din.

As he started to whine, head back, eyes half-closed, sleepy-like, Mrs. Bitterman felt that this was all she could take. Any second, he'd go over the forbidden line of her resistance, and it'd be all over. There'd be a scene, she'd holler like a fishwife, everyone'd turn around and stare, and her face would be full red from shame and frustration. The helpless explosion was just beneath the surface. Her temples throbbed, her tongue held back, thick, dry.

Neptune's Cove Features announced themselves on miniature reddish-orange sheets hung on a miniature clothesline over the high, slanted glass case, the letters announcing themselves in thick white.

Fresh Skinned and Dressed
Farm Raised Cat Fish—2.19lb.
Live Rainbow Trout—2.89lb.
Fresh Ocean Perch Fillets—2.09lb.

"Look—Look—!" Mrs. Bitterman pointed, bending to Sammy's level, and a slice of beige fabric was revealed beneath her white terry cloth shorts; the V-necked, sleeveless top fell just over her middle and matched. The outfit emphasized her strong, muscular legs, the slender purple and green rivulets lingering over the thighs' fronts above the knees, and the backs of her thighs sprinkled with pockmarks.

Her controlled voice jabbed at him; her exaggerated eyes mimicked surprise:

"Look at the fish—. Aren't they delicious?!"

How would Sammy know, he couldn't remember tasting any? All he remembered as his eyes wandered in listlessness over the reflected glass, which mirrored lines of fluorescent lights, was his father carefully cutting a large smoked chub with a fork and a sharp knife on Sunday mornings. That repulsed Sammy. He didn't know it was a very large chub; it was a side of a fish staring up dumbly at him, not recognizing him. The poor fish was helpless on the old, thick white plate: leathery, crinkled, shining dully like copper. The fish seemed paralyzed, in shock.

Sammy was helpless, too, as his father daintily slid bones between his lips, which were tenaciously rolled closed. Then he pulled the hair-like bones carefully out, and aligned them on a special section set aside on the rim of the plate. If only the chub could talk, say what it felt like to lay bug-eyed on a plate, Sammy'd help. But no, there was no communication at all.

But Mrs. Bitterman—Myrna—knew her possible threats were useless. She wasn't the kind to carry them out, especially in front of all these people. Her threats were a soothing defense for her own pride, a reassurance of her feeble authority. Anyhow, she could only smother her son with love, hug him to death. She adored him so.

Sammy, still staring dully, his mouth opened to the size of a yawn, hollered out, "Chu—. Chu—!" faking a sneeze, even spraying out some wetness from his nose, and flinging his head forward toward his chest while doing so.

"Sammy—Sammy—." his mother urged, "Look—see the nice man? That's the same man behind the counter—he's going to wait on us next—. Here, hold our number and when it's our turn, you can give it to him—!"

Sammy looked to the paneled wall where his Mama pointed. A photo framed in bright blue plastic had a nice man staring back down at him, smiling a little under a sign that read:

Neptune's Cove Captain
Always ready to please you.

Yet his black shining eyes were startled. Was he to be trusted?

Myrna shoved the yellow tab between Sammy's first and second fingers; then she squeezed his little hand.

"See? There's mackerel—and trout and silver bass and wall-eyed pike and scallops—."

Her voice, tinged with desperation, had a singsong lecturingness to it. Her eyes and her smile sparkled.

Sammy's light blue eyes roved from the picture to the man, to the fish behind the glass. When his mother stopped at, "scallops," his eyes stopped, too. He yanked her pointing finger away. She winced. Then she croaked out a one-syllable laugh.

"Look," he pointed now, "they look like buttons."

"Where, where?" she asked. "Oh—yes—yes. They do, they do," she uttered, and exactly as she clapped her hands delightfully, prayer-like, the man behind the counter bellowed deeply,

"Savandy four?"

He surveyed the crowd, pacing back and forth behind the counter, his eyes not really stopping anywhere—.

"S-s-savandy four—savandy four," and then he stopped, his arm stretched backward and his fingers on the invisible button that would change the large, digital-like clock sign to seventy-five.

"Here! Here!" Myrna answered, breathless, following him and vying for his attention.

"Here, Sammy," and she picked up her son under the little armpits, her shoulder-strapped, pouch-like purse falling heavily down her arm to the crease of her elbow, and he stretched awkwardly, and squirming, gave the man the number.

The man smiled nicely, taking it.

"Thanks, Sammy."

His eyes kidded, twinkling. Sammy was put back down abruptly.

"Let's see—." With part of her hand on her chin, and the other hand on a hip, purse swinging, Myrna hurriedly entered a world which eliminated her son, but Sammy felt its importance touching him.

"H-m-m—. The smelts are cheap—seventy-nine cents a pound? We've never tried them—."

The man rested his arm on top of the counter so the fingers hung over. He swiped his opaque lips across his shoulder as it rose to meet them, exposing a pink smudge on the sprinkled uniform. He put his other hand on his hip and stomped a foot lightly, so that his posture rose.

"Are they from Lake Michigan?"

The nice man nodded. He was featureless with light skin, black hair and eyes, and a pleasant, non-committal smile. Myrna's pale eyes lingered for a last protective check on Sammy; then she was gone, peering and bending between and beyond the weave of lines and circles of reflected lighting.

Sammy walked back and forth unevenly in front of the glass, leaning toward it as his index finger swept across. He stopped, inched his nose forward so that it rested gently on it, and the glass felt cold and hard and buzzy, like swimming underwater and it smelled fishy and was warm from the lights, and several piles and parts of fish blended close to him, changing themselves into monsters with many eyes on top of one another and body thicknesses jumbled in.

Sammy stepped back. The display formed a hill of clear crystal ice-drops, like in Alaska. The specimens were all arranged exquisitely, bared in neat, perfect piles, forming rows as each fish made a gentle arc of itself, a martyr to the pyramid which it helped form.

On the left, stacked in snow peacefully and nakedly, were the mackerel, like prisoners wearing their striped uniforms. The smelts had been dipped in thick liquid silver and placed carefully in a pile. The thick torsos of the fresh salmon were grey and thick and mottled. He could only imagine their heads, for they were gone, and the tails were tucked under the ice. The silver bass were staring bubble-eyed, dumbly. The Lake Superior whitefish were armored like knights, ready for battle, without a mission.

On the right were chrome bins filled with rows of icy pyramids covered with fish stacked onto them in gracefully curved postures. Sammy's eyes darted to the scallops on a hill's crest. They were like white buttons on his mother's corduroy jacket. The pink snow crab, crusted in splendorous frost, hibernated in another ice-hill's thickness, tucked comfortably asleep. The mussels in the row below were soft wedges of dark, mysterious wood, each a jewel box to be opened gently to find a treasure inside. The cherrystone crabs were the raw jewel boxes not yet stained dark.

Sammy tiptoed to the edge of the display, and to the right of it, in a smaller case, fish were suddenly moving, alive! Their black, dotted grey bodies swayed, their tails finishing each movement each time in a graceful flourish, and the swaying began again, over and over and over. Their rich full bodies moved gracefully, silently. The wedged fins fluttered easily, propelling them across clear water. Their mouths opened slowly; the pink-pale lips almost came together but never shut; bristles made beards under them.

"Aw-w-w!" the mouths echoed, muffled in the water. "A-a-arghhh!"

Sammy crept to see the side of one suspended in the center of the aquarium. He looked right at its eye, tried to get its attention. There was no recognition. As Sammy turned, trying for balance, the black disc darted slightly in his direction, riveted there, piercing Sammy's own eye.

Other fish fluttered around inside the case easily; one's eye was missing and the skin there, white; another's fin was gone, and the scales where it had been were very red. Many were compacted in the back corner at the top, their bodies languid, plunging into the water like huge drops of ink.

Then Sammy's eyes darted further to the thick shadow on the edge of his sight. In another bin, layers of lobsters formed a blanket of mystery. Cautious and still, they stared darkly at him, their eyes standing out on their foreheads, their antennas plunged out from their faces, and their claws shut by yellow straps wrapped tightly around them. Two came to him boldly, one climbing over the mountain of lobsters, one along the bottom, raising their claws high, one claw at a time in slow motion. Their tails were Japanese fans opening and closing, propelling, their antennas whipping slowly.

"Ah-h—h!" they moaned, in a primeval way, echoing from long ago.

Sammy leaned 'way back and turned his head and looked at the original case. The orange salmon steaks were immobile on the hill of ice.

"LIVE rainbow trout—?"

The man nodded as Myrna moved to the right, where the tubs were, ducking to look in.

"I'll take three—. Sammy, you'll have your first fish—."

She turned her head at him—. "Mama will make it real nice, just for you—."

The man came over and with a neat turn of his wrist placed the red plastic cover slantwise over the rim of the aquarium and there it rested, the triangular spaces making fresh air for the fish. At once, the rainbow trout scattered, then rushed magnetically to the surface when the man's two fingertips tickled playfully within the clear water, making little waves. The trout skirmished, confused, diving and rising, diving and rising, their tails trembling.

"Ooh—. Look—Sammy."

Sammy stepped back. The one with an eye missing went right to where Sammy was standing, then swerved suddenly and smoothly, to the corner of the tank. His good eye surveyed Sammy blankly, then he twitched slightly and went on to the back, his tail sashaying.

The man's sleeve was rolled up and his hairless arm plunged in. Three large bubbles rose to the surface and made muffled booms; the trout scattered again, and forming a single file line at the bottom, sailed around the tank. The man's hand was thrust to this one, then that, but each time he meant to grasp a body, it slipped out easily within the circle of thumb and index finger and scurried back in line.

Then the man brought his arm out, dripping. He shook it mildly and wiped it in a diagonal stroke across the bloodied apron. Back in his arm silently and carefully plunged, making a specific slice through the water. The water shifted in one large movement. Six more quick, huge bubbles gulped deeply: "G-a-a-a-l-u-up!"

The trout were now forming circles at the corners of the tank in twos while their speckled bodies swayed and twisted; their heads kept time to an unknown, delightful rhythm. Sammy smiled.

The fingers became exasperated, grappling, struggling. The cuticles were red-rimmed and ragged, the nail edges grey. The man lowered himself so that his chest was close to and horizontal over the surface, almost touching it as his apron gaped. His arm shot in all directions now, making frantic, erratic bubbles that mirrored grotesque blue and pink shapes. His rushing fingers careened into bodies but could not catch one. The trout, teasing, one by one, swam to his hand, then darted to the bottom away from it, and soared to the surface. From the surface each nosedived from one end of the tank to the corner of the other end, creating graceful figure eights. Over and over and over again.

"Dammit!" the nice man blubbered, leaning finally so that the chest of his apron became drenched and dripped, not before a trout's nose poked it sharply and was gone. Sammy chuckled as he saw their pale-pink lips smirking, the thin hairs of their beards flagellating.

"—in a minute, Ma'am."

"Yes, yes—." Myrna concurred. Sammy giggled, his little hands criss-crossed over his mouth, his eyes squinting.

"Sammy—don't—what's the matter with you?"

Myrna's confused and wary grey eyes shot from the man's preoccupied face to Sammy's, meanwhile pulling at his reluctant fingers.

There was a LOUD splash, as with one swoosh the trout soared out of the water into the air, flying free! Their tails fluttered, then spinned invisibly as the school steadied itself next to the ceiling over the tank until every last one had collected there. When the final fish had filled the final space, the leader made a swooping arc over the lobster tank, with all the rest of the trout following in graceful single file.

Into the cutting room they danced. Strong men in white aprons, trousers, shirts and tall hats suspended their work over the butcher block tables, bloodied hatchets in their tensed fists. They looked up, in awe, to see a line formation creating a singular figure eight across the ceiling.

Out the trout soared and danced and bounced and twisted and strained their bodies beautifully across the ceiling of the supermarket, under the strong fluorescent lighting, across orange-ticketed aisles 6, 7, 8, 9, and 10, over baking supplies, beverages, cleaning supplies and spices, toward the finger-smudged automatic In-Out doors. Every steel cart, cash register, checker and clerk halted as one solid body.

Silence. A bald man coming in, intent on his list, absent-mindedly slanted his body toward the door as if to nudge it. The door opened—thwack!—and as it echoed unexpectedly he looked up, startled at the noise it made in the unfamiliar quiet. He met the shocked stares darting at his entrance; then he followed their eyes to the ceiling.

The crowd of trout fluttered above him and again waited to collect itself. The twenty tails whirred, and with their bodies perpendicular so their mouths pointed upward, all in unison flung their heads backward to the humans standing about, the black discs of their eyes defiant. They paused as one body now, and turning to the precious opening, facing a world they'd once known, began to fling themselves out.

The sudden rushing of Sammy's padded footsteps from the back broke the silence.

"Sammy, Sammy—come back!"

Sammy jumped up and down, clapping his hands.

"They're going, they're going!"

The bald man strode inside, ducking his head.

In single file, in a single flourish, they swooped through the air and out as Sammy's toe tapped the rubber mat before it would shut, and the door whooshed open much more. Out they went. Just before the In-door flapped back in place, Sammy jabbed his head out into the space, squinting toward the school of fish to get a final look.

A red-winged blackbird was suspended alongside the trout, his wings whirring.

"See?" the redwing queried the leader in complicity and friendship, his beak pointing didactically at him.

"What did I tell you? It's easy—. You just DO it!"

And off he flew ahead of the groupings, to lead the way.

The aroma of rolls baking as one enters the supermarket wafted up to them as the glass door once again opened for a customer. In parting, they looked back finally, noting the long, vault-like windowless building with huge orange letters across it along the roof's rim, spelling,

"D-O-M-I-N-I-C-K-S."

There was a body shop on the corner to the south, with crumpled cars in the lot. Across Green Bay Road a luscious trace of forest of Trees of Heaven and Maples hid the railroad tracks of the Northwestern station. A tanned, slim woman in a sleeveless purple dress carried a bulky grocery bag under her chin. She trudged up the embankment toward the tracks and went through the miniature forest as the leaves seemed to part slightly from the presence of her to let her through. Then they ruffled closed, and she was gone.

It was a bright, sunny, cloudless day; the sky was clearly blue. At noon, it would be hot. It was the height of summer.

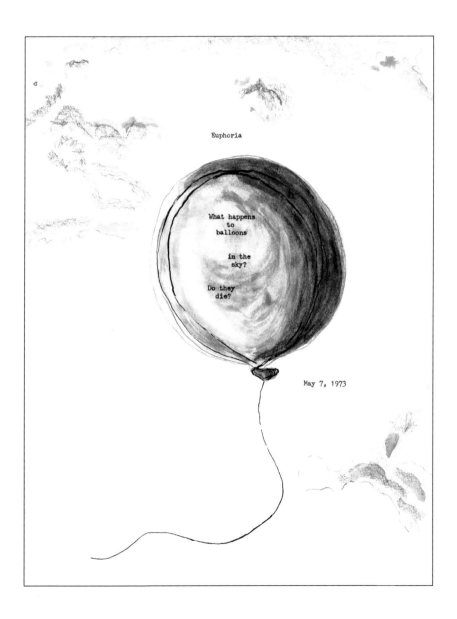

The Beautiful People

THEY CAME IN THE MIDDLE OF THE NIGHT. ARMED WITH THEIR GOLDEN necklace chains, and the two-toned Rolls Royce pristine under two thousand miles of dust, they came.

Dad, the finest and firmest of human beings, stumbled down the stairs quietly in his classic, soft leather slippers. As the lingering gentleness of half-sleep faded, he struggled to fold the belt of his brown cotton robe around his waist, but it flapped, anyway, over his pajamas. His sharp features were sharper, his face raw because of the sudden denial of his privacy, reminding us that, under his gentility were limits and rules and the rare volatility of his temper. Yet the gray cowlick stood upright, and the mussed, full head of graying hair kept him- - -always, always - - -boyish.

We, however, were alert in no time from a deep but childish sleep. We raced frantically after him, just like the hedonistic children that we were, obsessed with the pursuit of the unexpected.

It was three in the morning. The dogs barked and over the noise, the buzzing was insistent, impatient.

"What—the—?"

We almost knocked Dad against the glass of the storm door as he held the inner door open and we collided up against him. Even though it was a warm spring, we hadn't put in the screen yet, so we could see through to the outside. There they were, just a little beyond the stoop on the driveway, frozen like a photograph. There were the five of them, the five of us.

In the darkness, our bare yellowed doorway light spread an eerie small circle onto them. Dad picked up the remote from the parson's table in back of the couch near the door and clicked twice so that the lights on either side of the garage door blared and put them into the solid spotlight.

The mother was tiny and carefully compact. She smiled a sinister dinner-party smile with incredibly white and straight teeth that lunged at us. She wore white knife-pleated pants and gold chunks flashed at us from her wrists and fingers, and from her neck, spangled layers dangled to her waist. As she inched a bit out of the spotlight toward the stoop, the shadows and the dull yellow of the door light emulated her tinted gold hairdo, her dark waxy lips, and colorless eyes that were deep as marbles.

Just a little in back of her, the father stepped forward to align himself with his wife. He was short, her height, and balding. He too, wore white pants with sharp pleats that rose up to his waist under a bulge at his middle. The playful shadows made his chest very dark and as we peered closely through the glass, a glistening golden coin bolted out of a thick mass of black curly hair that filled the opening of a yellow shirt that plunged in a V to his belt line. Medallions like the one he wore were patterned all over the front of it. Spider webbed lines that sprawled from the corners of his small dark eyes showed that he was weary. He lingered impatiently, with his fists stuffed into his pockets.

The children waited in the background nearer the dark green hedges that ran all along our driveway to the curb and now were lost in the dark. The oldest girl stood behind them and gently touched their backs so that they moved forward and up closer to their father.

She had frizzy brown hair and as she passed through the spotlight's glare we could see that the tight curls and the reddish-brown tint at the ends were artificial. She wore sandals and a long gauzy dress that flowed as she moved.

The two younger children, about eleven and seven years old, had blond bangs and they wore white shorts and solid colored t-shirts. With their sneakers, they were tracing invisible circles on the driveway inside the weak garage light in impatient stops and starts. Then the youngest, a boy, bounced a rubber ball with sophisticated flicks of his wrist. The girl ran back and forth behind him with her arms outstretched and slanted like a bird or an airplane, looking at the door and smiling like an ingénue.

Then, all of a sudden, they ran to the stoop and hopped on and their older sister and their parents just followed naturally. They were now bunched so close to us that the glass door divided the inches between us and we stared back and forth.

The outside yellow light next to the door feebly tinged the smooth tans on their faces and on the children's legs. The mother had her fingers on the door handle in an instant and gripped it as gold charms fell to her wrist and tinkled like dull bells. Automatically, Dad's fingers shot to the handle in front of us on the inside and the lock clicked emphatically.

Then she said, "Obviously, you don't remember us."

I was almost as tall as Dad, then, and from his profile, I saw a glimmer of recognition. He clicked the handle, sharply, for good measure.

"No—who are you and what do you mean by waking us up—?"

She spoke business-like, in clipped words.

"Time *does* make a difference, I see. Surely you remember being in Los Angeles for our mutual cousin's daughter's wedding two years ago—. No? You *should.*"

Here, Dad's growing recognition made his gray eyes twinkle uncertainly, endeavoring to put her off.

"We sat at the same table, discovered we have a lot in common—."

She glanced at me—probably because I am the older son—then back at Dad, ignoring Mother standing vainly protective at the bottom of the stairs near him in her comfortable, nubby pink robe, which she has worn for as long as I can remember.

"You told us that if we're ever in Chicago—."

She swallowed hard, from distaste.

"—to be sure and look you up. We urged you to do the same if you ever come back to L. A.; but now, of course, that's impossible."

She waited. Dad nodded absently.

"Haven't you watched any T.V. lately—? Doesn't anyone in this God-forsaken part of the world watch T.V.—?"

Her husband placed admonishing chubby fingers on his wife's forearm, and either because of the additional annoying weight or because her long-suffering patience had worn her party manners thin, she shook her arm and his hand away, lashing out more:

"Dammit, it's happened—. Every damn thing they threatened us with—. L.A. FINALLY FELL INTO THE OCEAN!!"

She gulped hard.

"The danger we've been living under for at least the last fifteen years—. IT HAPPENED! THE EARTH OPENED UP FOR GOD'S SAKE! YES, THE EARTHQUAKE!! IT ACTUALLY HAPPENED!"

Then her voice calmed down a bit as she elaborated:

"There were fires, people screaming all over the place, falling into crevices in the ground and being swallowed—. Everyone is either dead or living in communes, shelters, even out in the open, right out in the open air, everywhere and anywhere—. You can't even tell where houses were, or highways—.

"None of our friends have room," she admitted, her tone dropping suddenly, her voice drenched with humiliation.

"Their places are either too crowded or they won't let us in—."

"What my wife is trying to say," interposed her husband, with his head tilted and a gust of softness to his voice, "is that we'd like to stay with you until we get back on our feet."

He added, plaintively, "We have nowhere else to go."

"You mean—" Dad shot back, incredulous (And then I knew without a doubt that he had recognized them completely.), "— that with all the dear friends you bragged about having in your life, not one of them will make room for you?"

Her desperation returned and she reached up swiftly to the handle once again, juggled it and demanded,

"Well, are you or are you not going to let us in?"

I never knew that a Rolls Royce could hold as many pieces of luggage as a Lincoln Continental station wagon, but it does. A stream of steel and leather suitcases paraded into the house.

Bedrooms were rearranged, people doubled up; there was much confusion. Mom and Dad gave the mother and the father the guest bedroom and Todd, my brother, and their brother, Johnathan moved into my large room while I chose to sleep there in the middle of the floor in my sleeping bag meant for overnight hikes at summer camp. Their daughters, Erica and Jolene, moved into Todd's room; he didn't seem to mind that much. My little sister, Beth, was comforted by the fact that she did not have to share her all-pink bedroom with anybody. Through it all, Mother was pretty together.

They were our cousins, all right, fourth or fifth. My father is a psychiatrist and two years ago we had all gone to Los Angeles to a convention of his associates. My grandmother had begged him before we left that we attend the wedding of a descendant of a cousin she had loved as a child and had practically spent every day of her life with. So, after our grandmother insisted to the hosts that we be invited, also, the odd, California invitation arrived in our mailbox. With our grandmother in tow, we all went on this unfamiliar journey.

I remember sitting at a huge table with the waifs who now occupied our home, listening and watching in wonder at talk of Jacuzzis and fabulous homes stacked in the sides of craggy mountains over surfs all named Malibu, and swimming pools as common as Chicago suburban hose water.

Their last name was Ravennus. The father was Barry; the mother, Ceray, pronounced with an "S," and the accent on the "ay," a variation, I suspect, of the original, "Sari." The children were Erica, Jolene, and Johnathan.

We spent a little time in the kitchen while they further embellished the horror of "L.A." We had watched the devastation on television and now, we were getting the raw, personal version up close. We listened in wonder, even terror, as the grownups sipped hot tea. By the time we got done, it was six A.M., and Dad went upstairs to dress for work. Mom dragged herself up to get dressed to face the prospect of a new day.

They stayed eight weeks. They fell into step with our lives. Cousin Barry pounded the pavements every day, looking for work. Most of the time he went down to Michigan Avenue with Dad where Dad's practice is. He was looking for "consulting work," he said, or "a managerial position," or "space in a brokerage firm." I never could pin him down, exactly.

The Rolls Royce, therefore, was left in our driveway most of the time. Some days, Mom found neighbors and strangers, children and adults, assessing it. That wore off, eventually.

Erica went to school with me every day. She was the center of attention; everyone was fascinated by her actually residing next door to Hollywood, but that eventually wore off, too.

We got along, and I liked her. She spoke very seriously when alone with me, but at school with acquaintances, she was boldly vivacious, almost hyperactive.

On our days off, which were sunny and bright because spring had swept in, I would drive Erica around, showing her the sights and hoping to interest her into liking Chicago. I took her to North Michigan Avenue, to Water Tower Place. On our way there, she sat immobile, her body turned slightly with her back facing the passenger door; she seemed to be contemplating a way out through the window as the sun highlighted the red of her curls. When, on one trip, I enthusiastically pointed through the windshield at familiar monuments to the city, she stared dully, glassy-eyed.

I get a thrill when, driving south from our home in Skokie to downtown, I turn the curve off Hollywood onto the Outer Drive, with the Lake on my left; the soaring skyscrapers going up to the horizon on the right; and an excitement grows as I approach the sleek sophisticated whiteness of the private boats bobbing quietly at Belmont Harbor. Then, when I come to the Lagoon, the waves in it are always dotted with early light moving on them while the men and boys are fishing.

It's something I tried to give her, without explaining, certain that once she saw it all, she'd be infected, like I am. But, instead, she turned herself slightly when I pointed at The Lagoon, her back still against the door. She gave a glance over her right shoulder, shrugged it, and her upper lip slanted sharply, in boredom.

Mom and Cousin Ceray went house hunting every day, up and down the North Shore: Wilmette, Winnetka, Glencoe, Highland Park. Mom was stoic, unflinching. She grew a desperate look about her eyes, though, that seeped through and made me uneasy, and which I've never seen since that time.

One afternoon, about four weeks after our visitors showed up, I came home early before baseball practice to change my clothes. I thought no one was home because only the "Rolls" was in the driveway. I ran upstairs swiftly, and the breeze gave me a surging feeling that someone else was home. Mom's door was partly open. I looked in. She was sitting on the edge of the bed, her shoulders heaving uncontrollably and her hands clasped over her face. She didn't make a sound.

"What's wrong?" I asked, standing there, helpless.

She threw down her hands and looked up at me, startled yet uncaring at having been discovered. Her cheeks were drained, and she allowed a tear to drip off her chin onto the bed and stain it.

"Oh-h—," she answered, not really looking at me, "I let Cousin Ceray borrow my car," as if that explained everything. Then she turned back, as before.

This must have been a turning point. Tension, like surplus oxygen, suffused the air in our house from then on. However, another four weeks went by before they left.

Their wardrobe was a rainbow of deep colors plucked from magnificent Polynesian paintings, a steady stream of jeweled shades. Fuchsia, Kelly green, orange, pink, aqua; purple with green stripes; yellow with purple stripes; knit shirts with insignias in even brighter, contrasting colors, such as a polo player on horseback ("Polo—. Ralph Laur-en," Johnathan said.).

They left the house each morning wearing sunny, soothing pastel shirts ("Knits—Izods—Bill Blass—Pierre Cardin—Calvin Klein—Hermes," Jolene told me); velour jogging suits; crushed Indian cotton jump suits; knife-creased pants; creaseless pants; strapless cotton dresses; and leotard concoctions with slithering straps and voluptuous bodices ("Adrienne Vittadini; Valentino; Anne Klein; Saint Laurent; Stanley Black," Erica informed me.).

They wore them carefully, with style. Cousin Ceray was constantly smoothing the corners of her lips with her index fingertips, poking them into the cavern of her mouth, patting her non-existent stomach, and smoothing her white-washed thighs.

She was busy with her quest, never veering from it, whatever it was. I taught her to play chess; she caught on quickly. One morning when she came down to breakfast, I was alone at work on the day's crossword puzzle from the Sun-Times.

"Oh, look," she uttered, "You're halfway through already."

She flicked on the gas under the teapot, then turned back to me, declaring with knuckles on her thighs, elbows outward,

"You're precocious, Tom; I knew it from the minute I saw you weeks ago. You're very bright."

Then she turned her back at me.

All of us spent hours sitting at the kitchen table, sipping tea and talking. It became a ritual. Everyone talked again about Jacuzzis, swimming pools, magnificent homes, surfing all year long, weekends in the mountains all year long.

I spent hours with Erica and her sister and brother. They were curious in a standoffish way about my elaborate miniature train system set up in the attic and my scientific experiments done in my room. They would watch me often while I worked and sometimes, I didn't realize that they were there until I looked up to see them staring, somber-eyed.

All throughout our being thrown together, especially around the kitchen table, conversations were vivaciously chatty. We observed; they talked (It was good therapy for them.).

Ceray bemoaned that the Jacuzzi was the first to go. The day of "the quake," as the term was now affectionately coined, they were all lolling in it, "cozy, gazing at the Pacific Ocean."

Suddenly, they felt a collective brooding under them, then a moaning tremor.

"There was no time," Ceray explained coolly, and as bricks and marble bounced and disintegrated into pieces below them on the curving road that led to their house, they whooshed into the air like geysers and ran, literally, for their lives.

They jumped onto their driveway, steadying their bodies to stand up as the earth vibrated, only to witness the unbelievable horror of the neighborhood's vast hills surrounding them—Beverly Hills—bellowing and groaning and echoing, like a resistant monster, enormous piece by enormous piece—slowly, slowly sliding into the ocean, chunk after chunk after chunk. Magnificent homes enormously resisted yet dropped like Monopoly sets into the Pacific and were gone; so did landscaped acres: trees, pools, cabanas, tennis courts, artificial lakes, golf courses, hotels, country clubs, Rodeo Drive, the ultra shops. The Earth Itself split open its vast jaws and swallowed everything.

Ceray spoke clinically about it: "It was ghastly."

"I guess we were saved," she reasoned, "because we lived on the highest hill and its magnificent strength hadn't given in yet. We looked way, way down and saw everything from there. I'll bet," she said with nostalgia, "it's still standing. It's our rock," she declared, and, with the greatest emotion yet, her tiny nostrils flared.

"We have (had) a fabulous house in the mountains, a Jacuzzi, a Rolls," was the litany.

"What else is there?" my father would josh warmly, on a rare moment.

"And—," she would go on, unheeding, "Chicago is a rotten place to live—the weather—and all—."

And here she would flutter her iridescent manicured nails like butterfly's wings, dismissing the four million inhabitants, the city and its outlying suburbs into sawdust.

It was early summer. Dad came in alone just before dinner to find me watching the six o'clock news on our portable television set in the kitchen. As always, I eagerly rushed to greet him with bits of the day's information.

"Bill Kurtis just announced that within ten years the weather on the West Coast is going to be reversed with ours. *They're* going to have freezing storms, and *we're* going to have sun most of the time!"

I clapped my hands raucously, and laughed, expectant: "Can't you just *imagine* the exodus??!!!"

Dad had taken off his suit jacket before coming in and a raised index finger was in the collar so that the grey jacket was draped over his shoulder. He had looked weary from work and the drive home.

After my announcement his eyes twinkled and I knew that he was lingering on the image of that early spring morning when the cousins had arrived.

One morning, while all of us sat around our kitchen table made larger by the insertion of matching leaves that we had never used before (and will never need to use again), they announced that they really should leave, even though they had not found a place to live. I was really touched when Ceray's whole face softened and her voice actually had a lilting edge to it when she declared how thankful they all were because of our incredible kindness.

They packed their bags (Gucci, Bottega Veneta) and were gone by seven the next morning. They were going to stay at the North Shore Hilton. It has an indoor-outdoor pool. We all stood on the stoop and waved good-bye as the Rolls Royce backed cleanly down the driveway and their hands fluttered out the windows. Mom was in her pink robe, her face drained, but her eyes were clear. Dad was rocking back and forth on his heels, a thin line of a smile on his face, flushed with an odd mixture of relief and pride.

They came for dinner once or twice after that. We haven't seen them since. It's been two years. A month after they left a crystal wine decanter with a long goose neck arrived from Neiman Marcus ("Waterford," my mother says.).

"Thanks for everything!" the grey and white calling card discreetly hailed us.

Word came through my grandmother that they have settled in a stately old house on the Lake in Glencoe, but are "looking to buy" in Lake Forest, and are having trouble doing that. They're patient, my grandmother says. She added that Cousin Barry is a full-time consultant for an advertising firm on North Michigan Avenue.

We haven't been invited for dinner, yet. In spite of it all, I wish we could see them more. After all, they are our relatives, our own flesh and blood.

Rice Paper

We are on our first trip to Hawaii. We are yearning for a taste of Paradise.

We have visited the Polynesian Village, Pearl Harbor, and the Dole Plantation. We are enthralled that people from cultures from all around the world are tourists, just like us. We have only known their unusual ways and unfamiliar modes of dress from afar in movies and newspaper photographs, and here they are, up close.

Going to and from the elevators, I am compelled to look up with fascination at the squared translucent rice paper fans, hung in rows from the ceiling, swaying slowly forward and backward in even rhythm, a contrived touch of Paradise, a modern trace of a primitive way of life, now gone.

The tall, sleek elevator doors bounce heavily and come to rest, and then whoosh open.

I step in. I push "32."

The platinum doors smoothly begin to close; then, as if startled, the panels tremble and fling apart. Two Japanese men rush in, and bow slightly. I nod.

Up to "12."

The doors open. Three Japanese women step in tentatively, bow to the men, smiling. I back up a bit to make more room.

Next, "15."

Doors open. Three more Japanese women rush in. Just after the doors close, they bow sweetly, then turn around to face the front, smiling and chattering in low tones. I move slightly to the rear.

Then, "17."

Two Japanese men enter while in business-like conversation with one another. They instantly stop to acknowledge the passengers, nodding as they grin and chuckle. The women giggle softly, bow in unison, then shift, getting comfortable alongside one another.

I take one large step back, my shoulder blades now flush against the elevator wall, watching. I am on the outside looking in. I am invisible.

The consistent chattering now has a humming, lyrical quality, women smiling, heads nodding, men keeping to themselves.

"20:" Ding.

Doors open. Still chattering, all get off at once, as if they are going to an important meeting together. I sigh, anticipating relief, and step forward, grateful for having been given the luxury now of the full space inside of the elevator.

Now, as one entity, outside the doors on stable flooring, the group suddenly stops short, turns to face me, smiling greatly and sincerely delighted; and with assertive, justified pride, bow and bow and bow. It is as though the elevator doors have paused to accommodate them.

I am stunned. They knew I was there? But I was invisible!! How could they know of my presence? My heart bursts. I want to laugh, to shout, to yell with hearty joy.

They still face me, dressed in tourist suits and dresses, as if patiently waiting for me to give some kind of signal so that they can move on.

And then the doors snap closed.

Keeping Up With the Joneses

A SHORT AND STOCKY MAN WITH A DARK COMPLEXION STOOD OUTSIDE in front of his suburban ranch-style house on a summer evening after dinner, enjoying the scenery. He folded his arms comfortably across his chest, his feet apart and stapled onto the newly finished driveway. His house was recessed from the street, and so he looked at the fronts of the block of homes next to his that went on and ended at the curb, pleased by the length of his Kelly green front lawn in comparison to theirs.

Catty-cornered across the street his neighbor, Mr. Smith, thin and blond and of average height, emerged from the doorway on the side of his tri-level house, stopping at the curb of his long driveway, his toes jutting over just a bit. He put his hands in his pockets, clicked his tongue absentmindedly and sighed. He looked upward to allow the light breeze to stroke his face, at the same time savoring the unique aroma of the beginning of summer.

Looking across the street simultaneously, they greeted one other, Mr. Jones grunting and Mr. Smith nodding.

"The summer is finally here," he offered.

"Yeah."

"It's hard to believe that just a week-and-a-half ago, it was forty degrees and we were wearing jackets."

Mr. Smith looked forward to his wife diligently planting bright red impatiens between the purple berry bushes under the front windows. He would be eager to watch each flower grow slowly, spreading more and more into its own little bouquet and then blend with all the multitude into one magnificent carpet of red while the summer ambled on slowly, too. He marveled, every year, that each blossom was ultimately important and necessary and that, if even one disappeared, there would be an empty space and the wholeness of it would be incomplete.

"Hey-y-y—if you need to, you can borrow my new gas lawn mower. The best, the top a' the line. Bright red. Fifty dollars, just came out."

"Thanks, but ours is still doing good. I thought that the mowers were all sold out, everywhere. Where did you find yours?"

Mr. Jones winked and chuckled heartily.

"There's a special wholesale place that our cousin got us into. He's in the hardware business."

Mr. Smith's eyes wandered to the nubile maple tree that stood in the center of his neighbor's lawn; the leaves gasped within the tiny breeze, barely moving.

"We're gettin' a brand new Grand Prix."

There were already two cars parked in front, one, a grayish blue Buick; the other an oversized black Lincoln Continental.

Mr. Smith's friendly brown eyes darted back, and he smiled. Under the bravado, he detected the vulnerability of his neighbor.

"Yeah?"

Mr. Jones's face flushed with excitement.

"I love the Buick, but we're gonna trade it in. The exciting part is—"

Then, as if he could not contain his emotions, his raw voice revved up and his brown eyes glistened.

"—they're gonna special order the Grand Prix in a brand new color they're offering, a real—-nice—-pale—yellow—"

And here, his tone slowed and his thick arm slowly rose and stretched to his side for emphasis.

"lemon—they call it—.

"My wife doesn't want to buy it. She says it's too expensive at four and a half thousand dollars, a luxury that we can't afford and we don't need it. I think the bright color embarrasses her. She'll get used to it."

And he nodded and chuckled, rocking back and forth from his heels to his toes, making clacking sounds with his tongue.

"Well—." Mr. Smith responded, groping for something to say.

"We had our linoleum floor in the kitchen replaced. We now have the newest kind of tile floor that has permanent coating on top of it so that it doesn't ever have to be waxed."

"—And it has bucket seats—."

"Wh-a-at?? My floor has bucket seats?"

"Na-a-h-h—," Mr. Jones rebuffed in his gravelly voice, flinging his arm at Mr. Smith.

"—My Grand Prix—it has BUCKET SEATS!"

And he abruptly thrust his fists into his pockets, turned swiftly and strutted unevenly down the pink faux brick driveway that led to his stained glass front door. He started to trip when he got to the stoop, re-balanced himself, stepped up and rushed inside and slammed the door, making a rich echoing sound like a cannon soaring toward the enemy.

Mr. Smith's shoulders fell gently as he turned to go back into his home, although the evening's darkness had not yet fallen to close the day. As he walked up his cement driveway, his fingers fluttered vaguely. Just before he mounted the little stoop, he paused and turned to watch the two familiar blue jays bouncing toward the seeds that he had set out for them around the newly planted sunburst honey locust tree in front, next to the curb, a house gift from his wife's Uncle Joey.

Then he went in, crossed the threshold as he hollered upstairs to his wife who was reorganizing drawers in the bedroom,

"Wanna hear something funny—?"

The Candy House

Somewhere, there is a gingerbread house iced in bricks of white with black licorice shutters and flat chewy-red sugar slices filling the windows that are framed in white frosting. In the front, two shiny red licorice doors are side by side, welcoming visitors in letters of golden ribbon; "ENTER" on the right, the recessed door hugged by a thin dark chocolate shadow; and "EXIT" on the left, with its own salted pretzel arch above it. Tall posts of black candy sticks stand like sentries on either side of the doors, crowned with stiff sugar ribbon candy lampshades and large yellow jelly bean bulbs inside each one. A cottage house with a striped peppermint-green steeple and a chocolate almond bark-tiled roof is attached at the right end, its stones made of macadamia chips and maple syrup mortar pressed between.

A cluster of tiny brass bells chirp from above when the entry door is pushed inside. The upper half of a white wooden door opposite the entrance is opened to reveal a woman in a long old-fashioned white working dress that billows as she leans over a large porcelain vat filled with thick fudge soup, gripping a giant wooden spoon, stirring, stirring in a lyrical, sweeping rhythm.

The dark red carpet reflects the holiday, boosting the warmth that has been filling the candy house all the while. It is scattered with shining paper bits that have been crushed and tossed by careless fingers.

Red flannel stockings and plastic swags of holly hang overhead. Florescent rays pour down from effervescent ceiling lights, soaking into the surfaces of two glass cases that together form the shape of an L. Through the glow, from end to end, images of little ceramic figurines seep through from the shelves: angels in white with their mouths pursed in song; capricious Santa elves in green with yellow collars; little girl angels, in long red coats trimmed with white fur at the wrists and at their hoods; and angels with gold-tipped wings, holding wreaths or candy canes or presents. One stoic angel endures a crack at her neck!

White wicker baskets with crepe paper bows of red and green are lined up at eye level on the counter. On the shelf underneath, hardened fudge squares are trapped inside cellophane wrappings. Maple nut. Light chocolate. Dark chocolate. Boxes wrapped in red and green plaid are stacked high against the opposite wall.

Behind the glass, matronly saleswomen in mellow pink uniforms and netting wrapped tightly onto their hair like bathing caps scoot back and forth, smiling endearingly, their voices twinkling. A saleslady with hair dyed dark and slim painted lips lines little white accordion-pleated cups on the workspace in front of her, her floury fingers playing inside them, making sweet crinkling sounds while she prepares to fill the silky white boxes. Chocolate mothballs. Pink-and-white peppermint squares. Chocolate-and-mint-green-striped squares.

She looks up quickly in spurts at a tall, thin young woman watching her on the other side and says,

"Fudge balls- - creams- -gooey, rich-like," as if she were enjoying eating them right there.

The young woman has silky blond hair that is up in a soft bun. Her patient voice hums "mmmm-hmmm," in understanding.

Way down beyond the entrance, there is a fireplace of dark red brick with tools of black iron leaning on its side. In front of the screen, an inviting white painted rocking chair is decorated for the holiday with a green and red plaid seat cushion and large red bows between the slats.

A tall, hefty gentleman contemplates the presents displayed snugly under a Christmas tree in the corner. He has a round full face; a white, fluffy beard; shining rosy cheeks puffed to bursting like holiday buns rising in the oven from the warmth inside it; a red and green plaid flannel shirt; blazing red suspenders clipped at the waist of plump, chamois trousers; and black rubber boots bulging at the tips. He has been drawn to the presents by the colorful wrappings: snowmen dancing across a pale blue sky; a sophisticated box shining in solid red.

Gradually, the crowd mushrooms. Each customer has backed away politely into the growing throng after having tugged a label with a number on it from the mouth of the shiny red plastic device on the counter top of the cross section of the candy cases.

And so, they wait.

A woman in an old mouton coat and a knit cap pulled down over her ears is mesmerized by the ceramic figures in the glass case as she bends to look closely at them. Nearby, two elderly women in raincoats and clunky black shoes huddle close to the rows of candies. The thin, taller of the two slowly pulls off her plastic bonnet and its dewdrops sprinkle a halo overhead, while her friend self-consciously pats her delicate white scarf all around her head to keep it set in place. Close to the three of them, a short woman with a man's haircut the color of dulled steel barks in a highly pitched voice at no one in particular.

There are broad-shouldered men in lumber jackets impatiently pacing up to the front from out of the crowd and reluctantly settling back in again to while away the time with idle chatter. A young woman with the ruddiness of winter across her face is nervously rocking back and forth on her tiptoes in an outfit that is too light for this weather: flared cotton jeans, gym shoes and a short patterned jacket.

The hefty man in the plaid shirt and suspenders has come over to mingle with the customers and now he and a plump saleslady are conferring in front of the barely visible doorway to the stock room. While he sets back a little on his heels with obvious enjoyment, his hearty cheeks glowing even fuller now, she is gleefully dropping crinkly translucent bags filled with all sorts of candies into the dark abyss of a rough sack: sugar-covered thimbles in cherry red, green mint, yellow lemon, pale white. Also, jelly beans; white-coated pretzels, dribbled with red and green icing; small striped peppermint canes; white mints swirled with red or green. Package after package after package, crackling as they flop deep inside, until the sweet pile reaches the rim. The saleslady wraps the top with strong red ribbon, then ties it tightly with a bow, emitting a little sigh.

The jolly man says, "I could not have done this without you."

The tinkling bells above the entrance bounce as two blond boys rush in wearing elves' costumes made of green and yellow, identical to those in the glass case. The hearty man chuckles in recognition. The bells on their toes clink as they jump to his side.

"You forgot your eyeglasses!" they shout, almost in unison, the taller boy waving a set of old-fashioned spectacles, too small for a man his size.

A red-headed man had appeared to be standing on a plastic box in front of the glass case, making him very tall so that his head is way above the crowd and almost touches the ceiling. When coming closer it is obvious that he is not on a box, that he is incredibly, incredibly tall, leaning against the glass so that his head is far, far above, enabling him to talk earnestly to the saleslady looking up at him from behind the counter.

Something has made him turn himself around and now, he is stilled, carefully watching from across the room.

"Come with me - - -" the plump saleslady beckons to the hefty man in suspenders, as though they have a pre-arrangement.

They turn and she opens the invisible door that leads to the stock room and they go inside.

The customers are now somewhat listless but still patiently waiting, dressed in down coats, cloth coats, raincoats, and jersey workout jackets. The warm holiday air inside has become stuffy.

A blond woman whose makeup has made her appear much younger than her age recognizes the youngest daughter of neighbors who had lived across the street from her and had moved away. The child had been the smallest and most delicate of the four children; her older siblings were all big in size with very dark hair and eyes and olive skin. Now, about sixteen years old, she has grown too big because she is still baby-like. Her face is still heart-shaped and small, as is her nose, her hair dark blonde and her eyes still purely blue. Her shoulders are broad under a large, puffy dark green down jacket with a contrasting gold diamond pattern that is too feminine for the bulky style. As a toddler, her hair had been curly and blond and her mother had always set her hair in ringlets every morning before she ventured out for the day. It is difficult to know if Barbara recognizes her; she now wears glasses that have tiny gold rims and glaze over her once-friendly eyes, giving her a flat expression as, unmoving, she faces her.

From somewhere amidst the shadows beyond the invisible door, the aroma of heated apple cider reaches into the room. Then, smiling grandly, the maintenance man has bolted from the stock room, the invisible door slapping backward behind him. He embraces a huge glass punch bowl that rests on his chest and he sets it down on a small table between the two rooms.

Cups with little soup handles spring from out of the blue, are passed around by the rest of the uniformed staff. There is a gentle raucous air that floats throughout. Sips. Heightened gaieties. The large mood has burst forth and permeated the room. Glasses clink to one another. Toasts proclaimed. Joy endures.

Having collaborated with her mentor, the plump saleslady comes back in with him and unties the large bow of the clumsy sack, and the mouth yawns open. The jolly man whips the crystal bags filled with supremely rich and colorful candies, then, one by one, tosses them to the crowd. Hands wave, beseeching. Shouts of joy erupt.

The tall, tall red-headed man has been alert. He has seen the hearty man with the fluffy white beard and red suspenders walking to the red exit door, opening it and going out quietly. He tells no one what he has seen. He glances to where the man and the saleslady were, now an empty space. He espies a small white receipt curled up on the floor, walks to it and picks it up to read. It is a list.

'Traditional wooden toy soldiers.
Lego sets.
A miniature train set, complete with tracks and an old-fashioned coal car.
Model airplane sets.
Jigsaw puzzles.
Girls' watches, with pink plastic wristbands.
Classic porcelain dolls: black, white, Asian, Indian, Native American.'

He cranes his neck and turns to face the crowd, barely holding back the urge to dance for joy. He has stumbled into the miracle of a lifetime.

"Hey! Hey! That was Santa Claus!!"

The crowd stops. There is silence, then a loud rush. All go outside, stumbling. Up and down, back and forth in front of the candy house. No sign of Santa. A rush around the corners to the back. A cobbled road from a nursery rhyme book has appeared, meandering from the back of the ginger house, piercing the horizon. Before now, it had never been there.

The two blond boys dance in steps toward the crowd from behind a thick tree. The woman in the mouton coat who had been mesmerized by the ceramic figures inside the glass case yells,

"They really **are** elves, not little boys in costume!"

Dusk has begun. Night is above the ground. Still, there is daylight where they are.

Up, up, up the sleigh soars and the bells tied on the bottom of the golden sled jingle as it zips, zips, zips away, away. Santa has put on his red coat and trousers and his wide black belt and is gently holding the reins, settled into his glittering sleigh packed with bundles just like the one he filled inside. The laughing, boisterous elves are now bouncing on the tip of the pile of glorious presents, waving their joy to the crowd. The reindeers, with red and blue and green balls intertwined in their horns, have already been hitched up and are leading the way.

ZZZZZZZIP!!! Popping out of the orange of the early night's sky to be cobalt blue in an instant, the image zooms faster and faster and smaller and smaller and then tiny, tiny, tiny, until there is a colorful dot that - — -whish! - - -punctures the heavens and is swallowed up and- - - - gone.

It is Christmas Eve. And Santa is on his way.

My First Fantasy

My mother was washing her colored cut-glass perfume bottles in her bathroom sink. I was standing alongside, my hands over the rim, looking in. The basin bulged and billowed with Ivory Snow. Her hands rising and plunging into the languorous waves glistened from the wet and the bubbles as she lifted the bottles up, one by one, from the mysterious depth. The bubbles clung above her wrists and slid down her pearl-skinned hands; my three-year-old child's eyes were drawn like magnets down the long, blue, wandering veins on top of them in their secret nakedness.

Holding the tall sparkling blue one, in her hands went, down to her wrists and her hands disappeared completely (a gently muffled knocking echoing up from below); now as she poked underneath, the short round yellow one bobbed through to the surface. Up it came, her hands swerving to avoid the froth as it drooled past her wrist, soothing her arm. Her fingers made a ball 'round the deeply intricate cuts of yellowed crystal; the long nails of her thumb and forefinger were darkly red and glowing.

"Look!" in a low, steady voice I proclaimed and pointed: "It changed color under water!"

"What—?" my mother asked, distracted in her woman's way.

"Look—. The bottles change color under water—."

I noticed on her face as she now turned halfway to me, looking down, not exactly looking <u>at</u> me either, the first of her tolerances of my childhood yearning for Magic.

"No—the bottles are only being washed—."

"No, no—. The water changes their colors—. It makes them different. The bottle went down blue and tall and came up yellow and round—and the yellow is now orange. It's magic under there!"

There was a slight smile and she said no more.

The bathroom was off to the side in a corner of my parents' bedroom so that we had to go through the bedroom to get to it. I was often by my mother's side as she washed the delicate things in the sink or did her heavier housekeeping, such as dusting, making the beds or vacuuming.

She would place me down on the floor in front of the foot of the bed. The bed had a yellow fuzzy spread on it, smooth and bumpy in places, looking soft as a cloud. From where I sat on the floor, the bathroom was always bright yellow, as if beckoning. It was a happy room.

Clutching a blue rubber ball, I would be looking around the bedroom, which always had a subdued glow in it. Fuzzy darkness settled at the bottom, and since I was on the floor a great deal of the time, tranquility was suspended all around me. I could look up and there was my mother in a blue and pink flowered cobbler's apron, humming as she bent over, her arms and elbows winging outward above the sink or vacuuming under the bed, crawling under it in spurts as far as she could, resembling a caterpillar.

There was warmth that lingered from my mother, having just placed me there on the floor with love and care. The floor was shiny in its reflection of the sun coming in. Gloating within her affection, I came face-to-face with the bottoms of all things, looking around with curiosity at the world and the world grew and grew. The glowing cloud of air filled the space of the bedroom, the fullness of it especially touching my heart.

The finest details of the overhanging folds of the spread came close and big, its knobs of full yarn, small moons in a yellow sea. Looking up and beyond the bed to my right, I could see the ivory curtains of the bedroom window dropping just below the sill, lifting lightly with the breeze. Through the window a block of sun set itself flat on the wall, dropping onto the bed. In late afternoon, Venetian blinds sometimes covered the window, making a fuzzy, stilled grayness as the sun's beams fanned away, neglecting it. The door to the bedroom was in back of me, and I felt its presence opened in welcome.

We were all friends, the inanimate things and I, sharing the secret that they each had a soul. (I can remember later on, standing in my own room, my back to my dolls sitting on my bed, flinging around suddenly, to see if I could catch them smiling at me in secret, or laughing, or making faces. I never caught them.)

All around, there was a continuous dark strip of shiny wood that protruded from wherever the floor and wall met. I used to follow it with my eyes, starting below the first of two closets nearest me and next to the bathroom; on to the bowlegged night stand legs along the bed in front of me; then, peeking under the bed to the other side between identical legs of the other night stand; under the windows; then, into a sharp corner on the window's side where a white painted desk and matching chair were set.

The desk always beckoned, and from where I sat, and when I had the courage, I would peer under it, where a large block of shadow was always there, unmoving, and all kinds of twisted funny shapes were inside it.

Continuing on, there was the bottom of the dark bold dresser with the exotic glass-framed mirror above it; then, at last, the journey of my eyes ended at the bottom of the frame of the opened door behind me.

I was entranced by the unending strip of wood that held the walls in place, certain that there was a sinister, secret world in back of them. In my imagination, I would feel myself bravely slipping into the corner below the desk, between the strip and the wall, a happy sensation, plopping downward to the mystery below.

That world had been watching me ever since I had begun to be my mother's companion as she did her chores. I did not trust that world, because it refused to reveal itself to me. In guarding every inch of it, I was preparing myself to be ready for the time that it would ambush me in an attempt at kidnapping my very self.

When I would go to sleep at night, my mother would come in and sit on my bed, the edge plunging down as she did so. On especially cold nights she would pull the cool sheets and the warm thickness of the blankets layered over them and rest them just under my chin. It was then I felt especially loved again and warm with the thrill of comfort against the smooth coldness down under my toes. I would squint my eyes and smile much, and my mother would smile back, sharing my comfort and warmth.

Once she was gone, and the door partly open, the hall light making a tall shadow standing at the threshold, I began to look forward to my dreams. In my imagination, I knew, I just knew, that I would someday slip through the slit in the wall under the desk in the corner somehow, and an entire world would open up once I went by, and no one, anywhere, ever, could see the adventures I would go through. I would be thoroughly safe.

I would be taken to a special place, to a special land, for as long as the night would last—which would be a long time, indeed, for the specific hours would have been perfectly planned—and I would dream my dream until it was time to wake up for the next day. Night after night I did this.

When the time was ripe, and unexpectedly, I slipped through the tiny slit. Down, down, down I went through the blackness.

Bounce!! Thump!!

HERE I WAS, AT LAST!!

A princess was curtseying elaborately to a King. Her face was made of porcelain, with a small mouth fresh as a rosebud. She leaned forward ever so slowly, her back beautifully straight, the long curls of her light brown hair almost touching the floor. Her golden, cone-shaped crown was very tall upon her head and dipped and thrust as she moved; a colorless veil covered it and trailed down, down, down her back, all the way and onto a vast floor patterned true to the aura of royalty, enormous diamonds each in solid black or white.

She was graceful as a dancer, keeping herself still so she could show royalty how determined she was, how respectful. All the way around the high stone wall people in elaborate dress were silently and solemnly watching her.

She wore a dark purple gown in velvet with a nipped waist and a winged skirt held outstretched between her delicate fingers. A wide lace bodice tapered from her fine shoulders so that it came together at her small waist, revealing a long pearl neck. All its details confirmed her beauty.

There were deep-red velvet steps leading to the gold-encrusted throne where the King reigned, his round flushed face reflective of undeniable kindness. The complete royal dress of white hose over taut calf muscles, stiff taffeta knickers patterned in yellow and green harlequins, a white silk blouse topped with a ruffle under his chin, and black pointed shoes darting toward the top stair; all of it contrasted with the strength of his rule over a loyal kingdom.

He sat tall, ankles crossed, fingers against his lips in eager curiosity, the palm of his other hand laid flat on the velvet rest of the throne while his arm was raised like a bridge over it.

In studying the aura of the gracious princess who came from a faraway land across the river, the King relied on the unshakable belief in his own gift of fairness while deciding any fate that she might ask.

The Desk

MY EYES DRIFTED OFTEN TO THE SPACE UNDER THE WHITE WOODEN desk in the dark corner of my parents' bedroom, next to the window, for that is where the dream of the medieval lady began. It was my mother's desk, although I don't believe I ever saw her writing from it.

A pale blue blotter with pearl-white leather corners was centered on top and to its right was a crystal ink well filled with midnight blue liquid. The sun's rays made little purple and green oily circles floating on top and matching prisms inside the slanting blocks of crystal edges. I would discover a neat scattering of my mother's pale blue stationery papers on the cloud-like blotter, with delicate, lilting scrawls in her thin precise script, short notes or words that she had written hastily to remind herself of something to be accomplished later, or prose that reflected day-dreaming.

When I was older, five years of age or more, I would come into my parents' bedroom on my own and notice that white painted desk in that corner of the room. I can feel myself now looking at it from a short distance, from the threshold of the door, upon entering. Here is where my dreams were set to rest, forevermore.

CPSIA information can be obtained
at www.ICGtesting.com
Printed in the USA
LVIC06n1245090813
347078LV00002B